SCORPION SCHEME

HOPE SZE MEDICAL CRIME 8

MELISSA YI

Windtree
Press

Join Melissa's KamikaSze mailing list at www. melissayuaninnes.com

Published by Olo Books in association with Windtree Press
Scorpion cover photo © 2008 by Robb Hannawacker
Pyramid photo © Wirestock Images
Cover design © 2020 by Design for Writers
Feline image by OpenClipart-Vectors from Pixabay

Yi, Melissa, author   Scorpion Scheme / Melissa Yi.
(Hope Sze crime novel; 8)
Issued in print and electronic formats.
ISBN 978-1-927341-84-1 (softcover).--ISBN 978-1-927341-85-8 (eBook)
      I. Title.   C813'.6

To advise of typographical errors, please contact olobooks@gmail.com

For the continent of Africa.

I've swum in the Nile and surfed off the shores of South Africa, and I still have so much to learn.

Do a good deed and throw it into the sea.

— The Egyptian Book of the Dead

I haven't come to you empty handed: I bring you poetry as great as yours but in another tongue, ... I bring you Islam and Luxor and Alexandria ... and date-palms and silk rugs and sunshine and incense and voluptuous ways ...

— Ahdaf Soueif, *In the Eye of the Sun*

Life is very hard. The only people who really live are those who are harder than life itself.

— Nawal El Saadawi, Egyptian feminist writer and psychiatrist

1

WEDNESDAY

Ninety minutes before our world screeched to a standstill, I hauled my suitcase outside the Cairo International Airport and squinted as the Egyptian desert wind desiccated my eyeballs and whipped the ends of my black hair into my face.

John Tucker laughed and pushed a strand behind my ear. "You okay?"

"I'm alive." Hard to believe that we'd landed safely on the opposite side of the world from Canada, near the only remaining seventh wonder of the ancient world. I didn't want to jinx it.

"*I am magnificent!*" Tucker spread his arms wide, relishing the mild January afternoon sun. Not to mention his own magnificence.

I leaned back to make sure he didn't knock off my glasses, but I couldn't help smiling and shaking my head at the pale skin of his neck and his wheat blond hair. Sometimes, I found it hard to believe that I'd ended up with such a milky dude.

Tucker called up to the wisps of clouds in the blue sky overhead, "We could climb Mount Sinai! We could visit the Valley of Kings and Queens!"

I adjusted the back pack straps digging into my shoulders and double-checked the suitcase between my legs. "We could figure out what happened to Youssef!"

Ms. Isabelle Antoun had assured us that a guide named Youssef would meet us at the airport and that our one month medical elective would be perfectly arranged by Sarquet Industries, a health care software corporation. What on earth had happened to him, or them? I slipped my iPhone out of my pocket, checked my blank notifications, and called Youssef. Again.

Then I left a voice mail. Again.

Tucker kissed the top of my head while I sighed and hung up. He said, "He'll be here any minute. Let's get him to show us Cairo before we get stuck in the hospital. You know how I was bummed to miss the coffin of Nedjemankh at the Met last year? Well, it's being repatriated here next week. Plus we could go see King Tut's sarcophagus. He had *three* coffins. The innermost one was made of solid gold. Or we could watch the sun set behind the great Pyramids of Giza. We could rent a felucca and sail the Nile. My friend Reza says he knows a guy who could set us up."

"Maybe the Pyramids." They'd drawn me here, even though a free trip to Egypt sounded too good to be true.

Tucker wrapped his arm around me and smacked a kiss on my cheek. "Thanks for trusting me on this, Hope. A free trip to Egypt. How could we turn that down?"

"Free lunch," I said. As in, *no such thing as.*

"Gift horse," he replied with an extra arm squeeze. Meaning, *No looking in the mouth.*

Isabelle had refused to tell us why Sarquet Industries had picked us for a free visit. Why me and Tucker, two no-name family medicine residents halfway through what used to be called an internship?

Sure, she'd handed us platitudes about Sarquet's commitment to worldwide health through excellence in electronic records, patient registration and billing (snooze), Egypt's doctor shortage (true), and the relationship between Egypt and China (huh?).

When I'd told her that my background is Chinese, but I'd never been there, she'd waved the maple leaf flag. "Egypt and Canada have been friends since the Egyptian revolution in 1952. You will always be welcome in our country."

Right. But they weren't treating 30 million Canadians to a free trip. Only us. Very strange. I gave Tucker a one-armed hug before releasing him, minimizing public affection out of respect for a predominantly Muslim country. "It's weird that we can't find Youssef. You'd think he'd meet us at the gate with a sign, like in the movies."

"I know," said Tucker, but he closed his eyes and leaned into the sunshine, so obviously besotted with Egypt that I gave in and sniffed the air.

It smelled flowery rather than the usual stench of airplane fuel and cleanser. It smelled the way you might imagine Prince Edward Island might smell, if you only saw the red sand in pictures. Is it possible to smell the desert?

"Beautiful," I conceded, and Tucker's smile widened, even though he kept his eyes closed.

We must've taken a back door out of the airport, because I'd expected touts ushering us into overpriced taxis, but I only noticed a few men in uniforms, including two in military garb, who barely glanced at us Canadian tourists, the white guy and the Asian woman hauling our own back packs and suitcases.

But why, after a night flight from Montreal to Vienna and a second flight to Cairo, had no one come to meet us?

After a full minute of fresh air, I broke the silence. "You think Youssef's looking for us at a different door? Did he text you?"

"Not yet." Tucker frowned and checked his messages. "But at least we have our SIM cards."

Ah, the SIM cards. Shortly after we landed and bought our Egyptian visas, Tucker had led me to a booth for local smart cards to avoid roaming phone charges from Canada. The SIM cards took forever because they photocopied our passports and made us sign agreements in Arabic. Tucker had said that from what he knew of Arabic, the paperwork looked legit.

"Youssef will find us. I texted him a picture of us. He won't be able to miss your outfit." Tucker grinned, crinkling his eyes. "In a good way."

"In an E. Coli way." Pre-visa and SIM cards, while taking turns at the airport bathrooms, my toilet hadn't flushed properly. When I'd pushed a second lever at foot level, assuming that the wall button was broken, the toilet had sprayed me with water from chest to feet.

Luckily, Tucker had been waiting (and laughing) outside the bathroom with my dry suitcase. I'd switched into a fuchsia T-shirt, a red hibiscus sarong, and dry sandals.

"Tucker." I waved my hand in front of his face before he started to hee haw too much at the soggy plastic bag tied to my suitcase. "If we can't connect with Isabelle, Youssef, or Sarquet Industries, we'd better come up with a Plan B."

"That's true." He grinned at me. "Good thing I've got one. My friend Reza came through. His grandmother lives in Giza. He said we could stay with her tonight."

"Uh, Tucker, Isabelle sent us our hotel listing and the name of the hospital we'll be working at. Shouldn't we stick to the plan?"

'Course I would've been more fond of the plan if Isabelle or her designate had met us or answered our calls.

And I got tachycardic at the thought of having to pay for the hotel myself. Med school tuition is bankruptcy-worthy, resident doctors made almost no money, and my student debt literally kept me up at night. What if, in addition to ghosting us at the airport, Isabelle and Youssef transferred us the bill for the entire trip?

Tucker's slightly bushy eyebrows knitted together. "This is a better plan. One apartment in hand is worth two hotel rooms in the ether, right?"

My jet lagged brain took a few seconds to figure out that he was making a joke about a bird in hand, two in the bush, and maybe a reference to the burning bush while he was at it.

"Reza says his grandmother will love us, and she makes the best ta'ameya." At my blank look, he said, "That's falafel to you, only made with fava beans, and full of spices."

My stomach gurgled on cue. "Is Grandma expecting us?"

Tucker grinned. "And *that* is why you're the woman I'm going to marry."

"Because I'm hungry all the time?"

He winked at me. "Passion, baby."

I winked back, even though I was pretty sure passion would be out of the question in Granny Reza's house. Still, I adored Tucker's encouragement in my quest to eat any and every food. One friend's mother said she'd never marry a guy who had smaller thighs than hers; I'd never marry a guy who shamed me over my appetite. "So we'll take a taxi? I've always wanted to see the Pyramids. Not sure if it's near the zoo, but ... "

Tucker rolled his suitcase to the left. "The buses should be over here."

I'm not a snob. I take public transpo all the time. However, in a foreign country, schlepping around my toilet clothes and shoes, after travelling for 14 hours, I yearned for the most direct route. "How would we know we were on the right bus?"

"I'll ask." He'd already made it halfway to a line of blue buses.

Almost everyone at the airport had switched to English upon hearing his Arabic. How should I say this tactfully?

"Right. I am. It's just—" I gestured at my soggy sack of clothes, because who'd want to haul that around? Plus I'd been warned that guys may grope you on a bus, although not so much if you're with a man.

He pinched the end of his slightly long nose. "I don't think a taxi will get us there any faster than a bus, but I can get one if you really want, Hope."

Now I was the global warming bad guy, even though we'd both hopped a transcontinental flight. "Okay, okay. We can take a bus to Giza. But you have to make sure it's the right one."

"I'm on it!" Tucker tried to flag down the first bus, ignoring the fiancée trailing behind with wet rags (me).

I tried not to miss my ex, Ryan Wu, who would have lifted my back pack off my shoulders and hailed a taxi before I opened my mouth. He's classy like that. But I couldn't stay mad at Tucker, who was like a Golden Retriever, all but sniffing the air and wagging his tail at the closest human.

"I knew Reza wouldn't let me down," said Tucker.

"Yay," I said, trying to sound genuinely enthused. I mean, after all, if it hadn't been for Tucker's worldwide network of friends, we might have had to crash at the airport. Was that even legal? I was pretty sure the Egyptian police would arrest hippie squatters, or at least move you to the closest hotel.

"Plus it's free. And buses are cheap!"

That made me laugh. At least he'd snagged one with air conditioning as a concession to my tender sensibilities. It was weird that they'd left the transparent plastic covers on the seats—you know how they cover sofas when you buy them? Like that, only thin, ripped plastic.

The driver, a man with greying curls and small, wire-rimmed glasses, waved me toward the seats.

Tucker spoke to him and told me, "Oh. We're supposed to sit down first and then pay."

Huh?

"I think it's so that we don't slow down boarding."

Too late for that, but when in Cairo. I shoved my suitcase into the first empty two-seater and swung myself beside it, my legs twisted askew. Although Tucker's legs ended up blocking the aisle, men carefully stepped over them, smiling. No threatening vibe at all, even though I was the only woman on the bus.

Passengers passed money up to the bus driver, who managed to drive and make change as he looped out of the parking lot.

Once we left the airport grounds, he turned on Arabic music, and several men bobbed their heads in time. I cautiously joined them.

As we oozed through traffic toward Giza, Tucker drummed on the empty back of the seat in front of us.

I stayed pretzeled into even less space than on the airplane, thanks to our luggage. But Tucker smelled good, more yeasty than usual, as I nodded off.

"Babe. Hope."

I murmured in protest.

"This bus ends at the Hotel of Horus. We have to walk to Abdul Munir Riad Square and change buses."

All I understood was "bus ends." I whimpered, but I shook myself awake like it was yet another night on call.

I trusted Tucker to lead me off the bus to the next stop. The Hotel of Horus looked like your typical extra-tall white skyscraper. A few brave palm trees lined the busy street. Three women in head scarves chattered and crossed the street away from the hotel and toward— was it, could it be—

"I think that's the Nile." Tucker pointed in the distance.

"Holy crap! The Nile River!" I couldn't see much besides cars zooming on a bridge and men talking on their cell phones, but still. I'd read *Death on the Nile* on the plane.

We bumped our luggage toward a bus station with a bright yellow and blue sign featuring a fit, bearded man grinning in front of a bus. People passed us, chatting on their cell phones. Cairo appeared not so different from Montreal at first glance, except the Egyptian flags adorning a smaller hotel's columned second floor.

Two young people in jeans and T-shirts listened to hip hop, judging from the music leaking out of their headphones, but more than half the women covered their heads, and a man with a long beard wore a full-length grey tunic. Cool.

The wheels on my suitcase seemed clogged with dirt and hair, which made it harder to roll over the paving stones under our feet and onto a second bus.

All the seats at the front were full. I nodded at a woman with four children. A grandmotherly type with a head scarf spoke impatiently on her cell phone. At least four elderly men dominated the front benches, their heads bent in intense conversation.

Tucker and I found seats near the back, but we had to shove our suitcases most of the way in and rest our legs on top of them. My feet practically rested in my mouth. "How much further?" I asked Tucker.

"Not far, not far."

Someone's phone rang. I didn't recognize it as Tucker's until he contorted himself to pull it out of his jeans pocket. "Oh, hi, Youssef. What? You're at baggage claim? We missed you, maybe because Hope got sprayed by a toilet—"

I straightened up, my eyes now open and accusing.

Tucker ditched his smile fast. "Um, Dr. Sze had trouble with the airport plumbing, and we couldn't get a hold of you, so we're taking a bus to Giza—oh, you want us to get off? Where?" He craned his neck. "I'm not sure exactly where we are. We changed buses at the Abdul Munir Riad Square. I think we're coming up on the Egyptian Museum. Hang on, I'll open a map—"

I reached for my own phone. Wow, Youssef! We finally got a hold of Youssef. He could drive us to the hotel.

I glanced out the window at the setting sun. No Pyramids in sight. I pressed the home button on my phone to bring up a map.

And I felt, as much as heard, a boom that rocked the bus and punched my eardrums.

2

B us windows rattled.

The reverberation thundered in my chest and, strangely, in my jaw, which twisted in its sockets.

Bomb.

Someone had tried to bomb us.

I knew it. I literally felt it in my bones.

Distantly, through my deadened eardrums, men shouted.

Women cried out.

Car alarms shrieked in the chaos.

Tucker tossed his body over mine, pushing my face into the back packs in our laps.

"No!" I hollered, although it was too late, and I could barely hear my own voice.

I tried to drop down to the floor, but our luggage took all of the available space. I flopped around like a sea lion plopped onto dry land.

I wanted to shove the baggage out of the way, but that would mean blocking the aisles. And we needed the aisles if we were going to escape.

Should we get off the bus?

Yes, if the bomb was under the bus.

No, if terrorists waited outside for us.

I turned my head to the side and tried to think, to listen, to hear.

I'd already lost 30 percent of my hearing from previous near-misses. The audiologist told me it could've been worse. Ears aren't meant to sustain gunfire at close range. Let alone bombs.

Fuck bombs.

Rage pulsed through my veins. I couldn't get one full day off before hellfire tried to attack me and Tucker through the walls of a bus.

I suppressed my fury to flex my fingers (yep) and all ten toes (functional). Great. No obvious holes in my head or chest. Party time.

"You okay?" I called up to Tucker. Hard to modulate my volume when I couldn't hear properly.

I felt his chin nod into my hair.

Okay. Good. If we had to run, we could run.

In the meantime, we'd tend to the wounded. Kind of our M.O. as M.D.'s.

An image flashed across my retinas: me and Tucker painstakingly bandaging wounds while our bus blew up around us. I swallowed and shoved that thought away.

"Should we get up?" I muttered.

I thought I heard him speak but couldn't understand it over the ringing in my ears.

Smoke tickled my nostrils. I pushed my glasses back up my nose and saw that everyone else had hit the deck. No heads blocked my vision. I tipped my neck back enough to view our bus's unharmed windshield. The glass on our bus's sides were intact, and none of us wore glass in our hair, mouth, or eyes. Trust me, I know that gritty feeling.

The bomb—at least the first bomb—hadn't hit our bus.

Not yet, anyway.

"I should call 911. Or whatever it's called here," I half-heard, half-saw Tucker say as he twisted his face to the side.

I nodded agreement, and he began dialling. His phone seemed to work. That was good.

I yanked my own phone out and saw I'd missed recent calls from both Youssef and Isabelle. Too little, too late.

An older man, his beard threaded with white, with slightly dank breath but kind eyes, spoke to us earnestly from the aisle. He wore a grey turban and caftan.

Tucker nodded when the man pointed to the door.

They wanted us to evacuate. I understood that, even though I still couldn't hear properly.

"Do you think there are any more bombs outside?" I enunciated carefully, both to Tucker and to our kindly man.

The gentleman shook his head.

"Do you think someone will shoot us if we go out?" I asked Tucker directly.

He grimaced. "I don't know."

At least Tucker was honest. And he moved off of me, which made my back feel 100 percent better.

"Well. They probably know post-bomb protocol better than we do." I stood up to join them, shouldering my back pack and grabbing my suitcase.

"Leave it," said Tucker.

You're supposed to leave everything behind during an evacuation. If you're sliding down an airplane chute into water, I can see needing your arms and legs free to swim. And I guess luggage will weigh you down in general.

Still, before I abandoned our suitcases, I mourned my one pair of jeans that fit perfectly and the brand new pair of black petite dress pants (stretch, so they were more comfortable than usual. They actually fit me off the rack instead of needing five inches hacked off the legs).

At least I had my passport and laptop in my back pack.

I noticed Tucker pulled on his back pack, too, before he fell into step behind me. As we snaked off the bus in a long line, I ducked my head down a bit. Anyone could shoot us through the bus's clear windows.

Tucker kept his hands on my shoulders as we inched down the stairs into fresh air and more shouting.

As my ears recovered (still ringing, but conducting other sounds as well), I heard frantic conversation in other languages. Sirens converged upon us. More smoke wafted through the air, and dust made its way past my glasses, into my eyes and onto my tongue.

From the outside, I spotted the real carnage a few vehicles ahead. A black bus smoked, some of its windows blown out, while bloodied people migrated into the street, their eyes wide with shock.

Tucker and my eyes met.

This was our calling.

They might kill us while we ran in to help. I'd heard of the two bomb technique in—was it Afghanistan? One bomb to kill and maim. First responders rush in. A few minutes later, a second bomb explodes to kill the helpers.

On the other hand, there might be no second bomb. And Tucker and I had vital skills that needed implementing. Now.

I nodded at the chaos. "I'm in. Just let me get my gloves."

I carry two pairs of gloves everywhere I go. This time, I'd zipped them into the pockets of my red fleece jacket on the plane, along with other essentials like ear plugs and hand sanitizer, and money.

Too bad I'd shed my fleece jacket and therefore the gloves after the toilet sprayed me. I could picture them bundled with my other soggy clothes.

I pointed at the bus and told the turbaned gentleman. "My gloves are in there."

Tucker swore mightily, but he knew as well as I did that we had to protect ourselves from blood-borne diseases before we raced in to help, especially considering Egypt's scary rate of hepatitis and HIV.

"I'll go with you," Tucker said.

When we tried to reboard the bus, several people stopped us, including our gentleman in the grey turban, who turned out to be the tour guide and spoke excellent English. Tucker explained our mission in two languages, repeating over and over that we were both doctors.

Finally, two younger men hurried onto the bus and hauled both our suitcases out, which embarrassed me because it made us look like pampered rajahs who couldn't be arsed to handle our own luggage.

Still, I unknotted my plastic bag, unzipped my fleece's pockets and handed one white pair of gloves to Tucker before donning the other myself. I grabbed my stethoscope out of my back pack while I was at it. Tucker already had his stethoscope strung around his neck.

Tucker extended each finger into the glove gingerly. He's not a small, and the too-teeny gloves could rip any moment.

My stomach twinged. "I should have packed a pair for you."

"Nah. I should pack my own gloves."

True, but the fact that we needed them right away still struck me as deeply unfair. "Who knew we'd run into a motherf—" I bit my tongue. "—a *bomb* on our way to Reza's grandmother's house?"

"Who knew?" He managed to get his last little finger in and wiggled it at me.

"All right, soldier. Let's get a move on." I waved my fingers back at him, and we headed into the fray.

"Did your 911 call go through?" I asked.

"It's 123 here, and no, I'll try again later." Tucker pointed to the right at the smoking remnants of a car. The bomb had blasted through the vehicle and punched a hole through massive concrete "Jersey" barriers before tearing through this bus.

I flinched. "Yeah, let's avoid that."

Luckily, a number of people already headed our way.

One South Asian woman held her obviously pregnant stomach through her orange paisley sari.

I detoured toward her. "Are you okay?" I held up a circle made of my thumb and forefinger, with my other fingers extended, in what I hoped she'd understand as an international OK sign.

Then I remembered that white supremacists now use the OK sign to signal each other, and I switched to a thumbs up sign.

She nodded but looked shell-shocked as she seized the hand of her little boy, who sucked the thumb of his free hand. They seemed intact aside from a few cuts on their faces and arms, I assumed from broken glass.

We moved toward a collection of bloody people, at least one of whom lay on the ground. I knelt beside him, an elderly white man in a maroon shirt and corduroy pants. He curled on his right side, touching his narrow, bloody nose. His whole body looked so thin that I immediately thought of cancer, although the blood pooling under his head posed a more immediate threat.

Tucker paused, torn between staying with me or splitting up.

"I'll be okay," I said, and he nodded and crossed toward a young family with two kids. The dad struggled to hold onto his daughter while wiping blood out of his own eyes.

"Where does it hurt?" I asked my elderly patient, pulling an exaggerated pain face to make it clear, even if we didn't speak the same language. If he answered, that would help me assess his airway and breathing, the A and B of emergency ABC's.

The man stared back at me, breathing fast but not wheezing. His trachea looked midline and his chest didn't heave.

"His head," answered a female senior citizen with a not-quite-British accent. I noticed her topknot of greying hair and the same skinny nose. "I can't believe we came all the way from Johannesburg for this."

Ah. South Africa, then. I tuned into the crowd around me and thought I detected Afrikaans.

Someone had tried to blow up a bus full of South Africans.

I filed that away for now. The man still hadn't said a word, which meant his airway could be blocked. "Can you speak?"

The daughter asked him, and the man answered slowly, with effort.

"He says his heart is heavy. It weighs too much," she reported, her forehead puckered.

Shoot. Chest pain, although the man didn't look agonized as he dabbed his bloody nose again. I suppressed the urge to squeeze his

nose and apply proper pressure for him. He was unlikely to hemorrhage from a nosebleed. I needed a better look at that head wound
for C (circulation) and D (disability, or neurological injury).

"Is he short of breath too?" I placed my stethoscope on his chest.

My dulled ears, coupled with surrounding sirens and wails,
meant that I couldn't hear much beyond him panting in my ears.
Certainly no crackles or wheezes or heart murmurs.

The man's voice boomed through the stethoscope.

I jumped back from the amplified noise, lifting the stethoscope's
diaphragm off his chest.

"Sorry about that, doctor. My father didn't mean to scare you. He
says that he's always short of breath. He has smoker's lungs. Two
packs a day for the past few years."

Of course. Emphysema, or chronic obstructive pulmonary
disease, kills off your normal breath sounds. I could detect a whiff of
cigarettes, but bomb smoke and the stench of blood overrode that.
The take home point was that his B, or breathing, was pretty weak at
baseline.

As if to contradict me, the dad gasped a long line of words.

I thought I understood one of them. "Did he say Kruger?"

The daughter's lips twisted. "He's calling for my brother, asking
the time, praying, and talking nonsense. He's scared. Something
about a mongoose and treasure and I don't know what else."

The man shifted, and I glimpsed the blood coagulating at the
right side of his head.

I pointed to it. "Could you steady his neck while I examine the
side of his head, then apply pressure to the wound? Do you have any
fabric?"

"Good thing I bought this from a tout." She unwound the white
scarf around her neck, revealing a diamond necklace with a familiar
shape: ♀, which looked like a cross with a loop on top. She applied the
scarf to her father's right temple, making a face. "I can feel the egg on
his head—"

The loud putt-putt-putt of a motorcycle cut her off.

An elegant, dark brown skinned woman removed her motorcycle

helmet, shaking out stick-straight blondish hair like she was in a shampoo commercial. The effect was somewhat ruined when she began to argue with the man who'd been seated behind her. He nodded as he extracted an oversized camera from a case.

I turned back to check my patient head to toe without turning him, since his daughter couldn't stabilize his neck and staunch the wound at the same time, even if she'd been trained.

His trachea remained midline, and he didn't have any obvious sucking chest wounds, shrapnel, or lacerations. He was still talking, if confused. GCS (Glasgow coma scale) 14. Not bad. "I need to check your belly, sir."

A brown hand with Pepto Bismol pink nails thrust a microphone in my face. "Karima Mansour, reporting from the heart of the impact of an IED. This must be terrifying for you. How do you feel?"

"No comment." Probably she was right to call it an improvised explosive device, or IED. A homemade bomb instead of military grade. Not that it made a difference to my patient.

"How does it feel to be a victim of an IED?" The reporter shifted the microphone into the elderly man's face. He blinked slowly at her.

"No comment!" I snapped.

"Get away from him!" the daughter ordered so sharply that Karima Mansour shrugged and trotted toward Tucker, who stood a few metres away, ripping up some fabric to cover the dad's bloodied eyes.

"Bunch of vultures," the daughter muttered, losing her grip on her scarf. Blood from her father's scalp dripped on the pavement. "He's Phillip Becker, and my name is Gizelda Becker, by the way."

"I'm Dr. Hope Sze, Canadian family resident doctor. Just remember the letter C if you have trouble with my name."

Her father sighed as I unbuckled a giant black fanny pack with a cobra logo to get at his abdomen. "Mr. Becker. Does this hurt?"

No major abdominal swelling or bruising. When I checked his face for a reaction to my exam, he didn't wince, but his eyes sagged closed. He looked ... immobile.

"Sir?" I gave him a quick sternal rub, pressing my knuckles into his breastbone to make sure he was still in this world.

He flinched but made no sound. Uh oh. "Keep his neck steady while I examine his head." I palpated the temporal/parietal swelling, a good 10 cm wide and boggy, with a small, hard metal circle at its centre. I shook my head. "Can you apply more pressure?"

"Of course." The daughter swore to herself in Afrikaans.

The father winced, still breathing but eerily silent.

I pulled open his right eyelid to reveal a blown right pupil, 5 mm wide and not obviously reacting to sunlight, while the left was a normal 3 mm. I swore too, under my breath.

"We need an ambulance," I said. And mannitol or hypertonic saline. With a neurosurgeon and anaesthetist chaser.

Every sign pointed to a brain hemorrhage and coning. He could stop breathing any second.

On top of everything else, I'd recognized the metal in the middle of his head wound.

A nail head.

The IED had been loaded with nails and other debris, spiking this poor man through the skull.

3

"That was unbelievable," said Tucker, once we'd safely sent our patients to hospital, met up with Youssef, and locked the hotel door behind us.

"Very weird," I agreed, shoving my suitcase in the spacious closet and dropping my back pack on top of it.

"Nice digs, though, right?" He surveyed the king-sized bed and winked at me.

"Beyond nice." My family's vacations generally involved camping and/or sleeping in the car. The luxury surrounding us slowly permeated my IED-shocked brain, including the foil-wrapped chocolates on our pillows.

The bathroom seemed bigger than our entire apartment in Montreal. I admired the shower tucked into the bathroom's corner and a full-sized tub lying below a window with a lovely keyhole frame.

The choice of toiletries lined up between the double sinks knocked me out. Sure, shampoo, conditioner, soap, and lotion, but also eau de cologne, a toothbrush, a razor, and—get this—a vanilla candle.

For some reason, the candle brought tears to my eyes. Maybe we'd get to enjoy our month in Egypt after all.

I texted my family a photo of the desk, complete with a complimentary notebook and two silver pens. *We made it to our hotel room! Love you, Mom, Dad, Kevin, and Grandma. Good night.*

Ottawa's time zone lingered six hours behind us, but my dad or Kevin, my nine-year-old brother, might have picked up on the IED. Right now, I'd marked myself as safe. That was enough.

Good Wifi, I thought, and started to text my ex, Ryan Wu, before I remembered that he'd blocked my number. Ryan probably prayed nightly that I'd hemorrhage gonorrhea and chlamydia from the eyeballs down.

"You need a shower?" Tucker plunked his butt on the mahogany desk chair, pulled off his shoes, and nodded at the bathroom to the right of the front door, across from us and the closet.

"I need something." Something to stop the IED images circulating my brain. Washing off post-crisis was always a good idea.

Tucker plugged his phone's cord into a built-in USB slot on the lamp base. He acted like it was no big deal, so I did too, even though I was thinking, *Wowee! This place has everything!* "You hear from Gizelda?" he asked.

I shook my head and checked my home screen again anyway. Phillip Becker had been the oldest and most critically-injured tourist in the IED blast. His daughter, Gizelda, had taken down my new Egyptian number and promised to contact me on WhatsApp once her father was settled at the hospital.

Tucker frowned at his phone screen. "I haven't heard from the Mombergs, either."

The family with the injured father. I made a sad face at Tucker and tried not to feel guilty about mentally texting Ryan. *Miss you, Ry. Love you. Even if you'd rather I burned at the stake for eternity.*

Tucker got up and unfolded the luggage rack for his suitcase. "What are the chances that we'd run into an IED? They haven't had a tourist bombing since 2017."

"You told me." I kicked off my sandals and dug my toes into the beige hotel carpet. Its softness took the edge off my voice. "That was part of how you sold Egypt to me. You left out the part that the bomb killed four Vietnamese tourists."

"Only three!" Tucker flashed me a toothy grin. "The fourth person was an Egyptian tour guide."

"Yay."

"But that's the good news about today, Hope. They were relieved that no one was killed this time."

"Yet." *They were not professionals,* the grey-turbaned man, the tour leader, had said. His name was Muhamed. I'd taken his phone number, too, so we could stay in touch. I turned my head from side to side, testing my tight scalene muscles as I said, "It could have been worse. There was no second IED." Yet.

"See? Now you got the spirit of it. One of the other guys told me, 'You know how you have school shootings in America? We have bombs.'"

"Good to know."

"No one was hurt too badly. They mostly have eye injuries and PTSD and need stitches and glue, but they'll be all right."

"Except Mr. Becker," I pointed out.

"Yeah." Tucker picked up his phone. "You could call his daughter. I wish they were at the Cairo International Hospital with us so we could check on them."

"I guess the KMT Hospital was closer. I'll wash up before I message her." I yawned and reached into the closet for a pair of white terry slippers. They looked twice my size, but ... free slippers!

"I'll come with." Tucker's eyes gleamed.

I couldn't help smiling. This guy would do me on my deathbed. As I unzipped my suitcase and scooped up my toiletry bag, I asked, "What did you make of Youssef?"

"He seemed like a nice guy." Tucker grabbed his razor and moved close behind me.

I shrugged. "Once he showed up."

"Well, to be fair, the whole area was blocked off for police and ambulances. He had to walk in. And he did keep in constant contact once he got our Egyptian phone numbers."

Youssef had looked 30ish, with dark, observant eyes, carefully-combed black hair, pleated grey dress pants and previously-polished leather shoes. He said he'd missed us in the airport between the toilet incident, us exiting the wrong doors, and—this was the big problem —us changing SIM cards.

"Yeah, but I e-mailed our new numbers to Isabelle and Sarquet Industries. They should have figured it out." I shook my head. No matter how courteously Youssef had led us to the Egyptian Classic Continental, offering us dinner and room service, I didn't trust the guy. "But at least he made sure we didn't have to go with the police to make a statement on the IED. Points for that."

"Want to join me in the shower?" Tucker wiggled his eyebrows at me.

I laughed. "I should probably wash off the blood and bomb dust first."

"That's what the shower is for!" He dropped his voice. "Ladies first."

I blushed. He meant that he'd make me come before he did. Most times, he succeeded.

"Oh, you think I jest. But wait 'til you see this." Tucker waved his phone at me and pressed play.

A drum beat and a tambourine immediately straightened my spine. I knew this song: "Walk Like an Egyptian."

"Nooooo!" I covered my eyes. Total '80s night cliché song for our Cairo debut.

"Yessssss," he said, shaking his hips in time with the first guitar chord.

By the time the Bangles started singing, Tucker was shimmying his shoulders, showing off his pecs and biceps.

I applauded.

He reached for the hem of his shirt, and I bent over, almost barking with laughter.

I needed this. Total decompression. No time to think about IEDs or blood or the old man fighting for his life on a hospital gurney.

Don't worry, the turbaned man, Muhamed, had told Tucker. *Tourists get the best medical care. They pay for the best. Not like Egyptians.*

I shook my head. *No. Stop. Stay in the moment with Tucker.*

Tucker lifted his shirt, flashing me his hairy stomach before he turned around to swivel his ass suggestively on the chorus, almost like he was belly dancing for me.

"Woo hoo!"

Tucker executed the classic "Walk Like an Egyptian" hand moves, flexing at the wrist and elbow and pointing one hand forward and the other behind his back and away from him. Then he whipped off his shirt.

"Ay caramba!" I wished I could call out in Arabic. I loved the muscles in his chest and abdomen and even his slight love handles. The hair on his chest and back had surprised me after Ryan's smooth skin, but I'd gotten used to it.

Tucker spun around to pivot his ass a few more times before he reached for his belt buckle. Once he got his belt free, he waved it in the air before he drew me closer and tried to spank me with it.

The hotel phone trilled in the air.

We both stared at the phone, a fancy, white, gold-trimmed contraption resting on the closest night stand.

"Forget that thing," said Tucker. He flexed the belt at me.

"But what if it's about the IED?"

He hesitated. "They'd call us on our cell phones, not at the hotel."

"That's true."

He smacked my ass with his belt. I yelped.

But the moment had passed, and we both knew it.

The phone rang and rang, a high, brittle sound that filled the room.

No. Unfair. I hadn't even had a chance to tell Tucker about Mr. Becker's last words (treasure? Kruger?). And this was our time. We deserved silence and privacy and shower fun.

Still, I crossed the room to pick up the phone receiver with the tips of my thumb and index finger. "Hello?"

4

"It's Isabelle Antoun, darling." As if I wouldn't have recognized her lovely, throaty voice with a slight English accent. She'd invited us to Egypt, all expenses paid, and talked past my objections, only to abandon us at the airport. "Youssef told me you'd arrived safely at the Egyptian Classic Continental, but I wanted to assure myself, is everything to your satisfaction?"

I gazed longingly at Tucker. He bared his teeth at me as I said, "We're fine."

"What a dreadful welcome to Egypt for both of you. I hope it hasn't turned you off our entire country now."

"Of course not." My hand curled on the receiver. I hate when people use my name as a verb. *Go away.*

"I know you were supposed to start your rotation tomorrow, but really, I think it would be best if you took a day to recuperate. Youssef could take you to see the Pyramids. What do you think?"

Strange. "I thought you wanted us to start in the emergency room right away."

She chuckled. "Darling. Why would you think that? It's far more important to look after you and Dr. Tucker and establish cordial relations between our two countries."

"Um." No doctor or administrator had ever offered me a day off. They prescribed work, work, work, and for kicks, more work.

Tucker raised his eyebrows at me in a meaningful way.

I smiled back at him.

He danced toward me with the "Walk like an Egyptian" hands and a head bob, making me choke back a laugh. "I think we're okay to start working. My ears are almost back to normal." *Such as they are.*

"Oh, I insist. What a way for my country to greet you! Let me take you to the Pyramids. You want to go, don't you?"

"Yes, of course."

Tucker's legs sprang apart, startling me.

He jumped around so his butt faced me. Then he started twerking, rhythmically shaking his butt along with the song.

I almost screamed into the receiver. Especially when he reached for his crotch.

I frantically gave the throat-cutting signal, pointing at the phone.

He winked at me and popped open his jeans button with a kapow! motion.

Oh, God. He was such a goof. But he was *my* goof.

And there went the zipper. Another hand flourish, like he was playing the guitar chord right over a critical area.

I writhed with silent laughter. I held up my hand for him to stop.

Instead, he wriggled his hips against mine, shedding his jeans before dancing backward, inviting me to join him in the bathroom.

"Sunrise over the Pyramids. Such a magical experience. Something not to be missed in one's lifetime. Riding on a camel's back. Or horseback, should you prefer a more stable ride. We could commission it all for you. You wouldn't have to do a thing."

"Um." I couldn't think when Tucker whipped around to waggle his booty in my face.

"Or some people prefer to visit the Pyramids late in the day, when most of the tour buses have left. Next week, you must come see the golden sarcophagus of Nedjemankh, which was smuggled out of the country and recently recovered from the Metropolitan Museum of

Art. On Monday, the sarcophagus will be unveiled at a grand ceremony by the Ministry of Antiquities—"

Tucker grinned as I checked to make sure his front half was as ready as his rear half. Let me tell you, he was ready to rock and roll. A bomb literally could not keep this guy down.

"Sounds good," I managed to say to Isabelle.

"Which do you prefer? The Pyramids, the sarcophagus—"

I had no idea what she was talking about. "Could I call you back?"

"Oh, but darling, I need to make arrangements."

Meanwhile, Tucker encouraged me to strip and join him.

I shook my head at both of them. "I'm, uh, we should work at the hospital. Establish a routine. After hours, we'll visit the Beckers and the Mombergs—"

"Don't feel that you must, Dr. Sze. We already know you're a committed physician, and we applaud you."

Tucker pulled me in for a kiss. I gave him a quick peck that he immediately deepened before his own phone started broadcasting Arabic music from the depths of his abandoned jeans.

He swore.

"Is everything all right?" asked Isabelle in my right ear.

Steezy. Out loud, I said, "Dandy! Peachy keen!"

As Tucker released me to dig for his phone, Isabelle continued, "If not the Pyramids and the Egyptian Museum, then how about the Al-Azhar Mosque, which is not only one of our oldest mosques, completed in 972 CE, but one of the world's oldest universities?"

Mosques make me happy whenever I see their round domes. I like circles. I smiled involuntarily.

"Or the Church of Sergius and Baccus, where the Virgin Mary, Joseph, and the baby Jesus took refuge when King Herod slaughtered all male infants."

Gah. That killed my mood, along with Tucker taking a left into the bathroom for his call.

"Downtown Cairo was once called the Paris of the East in the 19th Century. Or, if you grow weary of history, you could shop, eat, play tennis, or ride horses on Gezira, an island in the Nile."

"Oh, that's okay. I know I'm here to work." Everything she described sounded more like a fantasy than anything accessible to me.

"Not at all, Dr. Sze." She pronounced my name correctly, with the "tse" sound instead of the simplified version like the letter C. "Please. You must indulge yourself. This is the trip of a lifetime."

I exhaled. I'd transformed myself into a test-taking, procedure-acing robot doctor. Then, when I came to Montreal and inexplicably ran into murder and deceit, I took on the amateur sleuth mantle too.

It never occurred to me that I might have *fun*. That this could be a *vacation*.

Tucker had done his best to sell Egypt to me, but my brain had subconsciously answered, *Yeah, yeah* while I figured out what to pack, if we needed vaccinations, and how to persuade McGill's powers-that-be to let us out of the country for an elective. (Truthfully, the last was a cakewalk. St. Joe's couldn't wait to shed me and my hithertofore unseen ability to magnetize evil toward their hospital.)

Yet here was the woman who'd solicited us and whose organization had paid for our trip across the world. And she was telling me to take time *off*.

"Huh," was all I managed to say aloud, when I pressed the phone back to my ear.

"Think about it, Dr. Sze. You deserve a day to yourself."

"But don't you want us to come and help patients?"

She paused for a moment. "The best way you can take care of patients is by taking care of yourself first. We don't want you jet lagged and stressed when you make important decisions. We want you to enjoy your stay, and our country. Please think about it, Dr. Sze. You can call or text me any time, and I'll let your hospital know. They're already aware of your difficult day. No one expects you to go to work right away. It would be inhumane."

And yet that inhumanity was how I'd lived my entire life. I needed to wrap my brain around this.

Isabelle had never given me a straight answer about why she'd recruited me and Tucker for a free trip to Egypt. She'd insisted we could talk about it face to face.

Now she didn't expect us to spend every waking hour at the hospital in penance.

So why did they want us here?

My cell phone buzzed. "I'm sorry, Isabelle, could I call you back? Someone's trying to reach me, and I'm afraid it might be about the IED."

"Of course. Whatever you need to do. Please take care of yourself. Not to mention that handsome fiancé of yours." She tinkled a laugh and bid me farewell.

I ignored the new call and popped in the bathroom to touch my handsome fiancé's back. He smiled briefly but didn't stop blathering on his cell.

I sighed and answered my phone. WhatsApp told me it was Mr. Becker's daughter, so my stomach knotted even before she updated me on the bleeding in her father's brain.

5

THURSDAY

The next morning, I disembarked from the taxi into the rain, still slightly groggy from a fitful sleep.

"You okay, Hope?" asked Tucker.

"Yup." I lifted my bag over my head as a shield. Who knew it rained in the desert? I followed Tucker and Youssef past the white concrete pillars mounted at the front of the Cairo International Hospital.

It looked more like a hotel than a hospital, to my inexperienced eyes: white, multi-storied, with rows of reflective green glass. That plus the surrounding palm trees made me feel like I was on vacation.

I shielded my eyes and focused on the upside. "I never thought I'd work at a hospital with palm trees out front."

Tucker smiled and squeezed my hand. "A good omen, right?"

Right. If you didn't count Mr. Becker's epidural hematoma and cerebral contusion and the cut-up Mombergs as bad omens.

Outside the hospital, I surveyed the taxi drivers, the families, and the black-uniformed guards with SECURITY lettered in yellow across their backs. Could any of them harbour a bomb?

No. I wouldn't succumb to the stereotype of Middle Eastern terrorists. I reached for Tucker's hand instead.

Youssef grinned over his shoulder at us. "Which tree do you mean? It could be a real palm tree or a mobile tower."

I stopped interlacing my fingers with Tucker's. "What are you talking about?"

Youssef studied the closest tree. "That one is real." He pointed to one near the sidewalk with grey/brown, flaking bark. "But see? That's a tower disguised as a palm tree."

I surveyed Mr. Fake, the concrete marked with horizontal lines, like a bleached, airbrushed version of a palm tree. Unease flickered in my chest. Post-IED, I preferred everything out in the open. "Why make your cell phone towers look like palm trees?"

Youssef's eyebrows jumped up and down in surprise. "They're more beautiful that way."

Beauty. That had never occurred to me, or any local politician in my lifetime. Jobs and efficiency, yes. Beauty, no.

And yet maybe that was a guiding principle in Egypt.

Inside the hospital, my eyes widened. So much natural sunlight! That alone made my Vitamin D-starved soul expand. True, the walls could use a fresh coat of paint, and I felt slightly claustrophobic at the sea of bodies crowded in the lobby, but its high ceilings and wooden front desk thoroughly shamed our home base of St. Joe's. Which doesn't take much.

We nodded at the security guards, stepped through metal detectors, and ran our back packs through X-ray machines on a conveyor belt.

Youssef's phone buzzed. He shook his head as he read the text. "Excuse me. Isabelle has a software problem at Sarquet. You can wait for me if you need an introduction to the head of the emergency department."

"We're fine," said Tucker. "Good luck to you and Isabelle."

I wasn't so sure, but I smiled gamely. After twisting down progressively narrower hallways with zero windows, we came through a side door to the main ER entrance. Tucker pointed to a triple-nurse triage station beside a series of registration desks in the ER.

"We made it!" I said.

I let Tucker bat his baby brown eyes at the registration clerks. White male privilege is a total thing, with extra helpings for a charming blond dude.

While the clerks giggled and fluttered, I rolled my eyes and followed the Dr. Tucker fan club into my first real taste of an Egyptian hospital.

My mind whirled at the similarities to St. Joe's—intense-looking doctors giving lectures to eager medical students and residents, X-rays and CT's displayed on computer screens, and even a familiar-looking electronic medical record system, although their EMR logo said Selsis instead of SARKET. The ER even smelled pretty much the same, sort of antiseptic with a whiff of pus.

Of course the differences popped too. A strong preponderance of brown skin, which seemed cool. Nearly all of the doctor leader types were older men. Most of the women, whether staff or patients, wore a head covering.

But the rest of their clothes made me pull at the front of my scrub top and wish I'd ironed it. Every Egyptian doctor sported a white coat with a name and specialty embroidered on the breast. The men wore ties and dress shirts. Females looked like they'd stepped out of Instagram. I'd never realized that the black outfits with eye slits could be made of silky material that was much nicer than the two sets of ink-stained green scrubs I'd packed.

Tucker switched to Arabic to hail two men in white coats who stood outside exam room 5, directly opposite the nursing station.

I glanced at the taller one in silver glasses, whose white coat said *Pathology*. He avoided my eyes. The other guy, short and good-looking, turned and smiled.

"Do you know him?" I muttered out of the corner of my mouth.

Tucker grinned. "Now I do!"

How annoying was that. I exchanged a few shy smiles with the women and asked, "Can he point us toward the chief of emerg?"

"He says, 'I'm sure he'll be here within the hour.'"

An hour? Dr. Mostafa Sharif was scheduled to ease us into our elective eight minutes ago. I checked my e-mail. Nothing from Dr.

Sharif. Sounded like a lazy chief. Which meant I might not learn as much. On the other hand, I kinda welcomed a boring day after the jet lag-IED combo.

Tucker switched to English. "Dr. Hope Sze, I'd like you to meet Dr. Rudy Mohamed."

"Rudy?" I held out my hand, glad I wouldn't muff up the pronunciation on that. "I'm Dr. Hope Sze. From Canada. Really nice to meet you." When you're a woman, you can't say doctor too many times. And they'll still mislabel you as a nurse and ignore your orders.

"Welcome to Cairo," Rudy replied, with a minimal accent and a white-toothed smile. The carefully-combed hair and blue tie tipped me off that he was probably an internal medicine resident even before I read his embroidery. He added, "I hope your second day will be better than your first."

Uh oh. Tucker must've led with the IED.

"What happened on your first day?" asked a woman wearing a beige head scarf and discreet but pretty eyeliner and lipstick. She was shorter than me and had a slightly large nose, but stood balanced on both her feet and seemed self-contained. Her English was even better than Rudy's.

I underplayed it. "We got too close to the Egyptian Museum at the wrong time."

"Oh, I heard about the IED. Are you hurt?" Her deep brown eyes catalogued both of us.

"Absolutely not." I tried to smile. "Hi, my name is Dr. Hope Sze, and this is Dr. John Tucker. Could you help us find Dr. Sharif, the chief of the ER?"

"Of course. I am Samira Gamal, a third year medical student. Welcome," she said, giving me a quick, firm handshake. She nodded at Tucker instead of touching him.

Tucker smiled and bowed back at her. Points to him. I once offered to shake hands with a Hasidic Jewish man at St. Joe's, repeatedly, before the man brought his hands behind his back and made it clear that any physical contact was culturally inappropriate.

Samira dimpled at me. "You can probably find Dr. Sharif in the doctors' lounge." She pointed to our right. "Follow the wall past the trauma bay, and you'll see the doctors' lounge, the one with the code on the door. The code is 1 and 5 together, then 2, 3, 4."

Easy to remember, poor security. I smiled and waved. "Thank you so much!"

"She seems nice," said Tucker, cutting behind me as a stretcher trundled past us.

"Yeah, she's cool."

Samira's code opened the doctors' lounge door. No one sat on the large couch facing a TV blaring an Arabic newscast. I surveyed the fridge, the doctors' mailboxes, the microwave and the empty coffee maker. Switch the language, and it could have been any Canadian doctors' lounge.

I slung my back pack on an empty hook on the wall behind the door.

Tucker texted Youssef and asked him to forward the message to the ER chief. "Just to let him know that we're here."

"Good idea." You never want to be late in medicine if you can help it. Too bad lateness is my jam. I glanced at the TV and blinked. "Hey, that's Karima Mansour!"

I recognized her straight, blondish hair, although the reporter had adopted an earnest expression and a dark smudge on her left cheek that reminded me of the marks football players made under their eyes.

"Weird. I thought she had an afternoon show. Oh, she's reporting on the IED," said Tucker.

Sure enough, they switched to footage of the blown-out bus windows before honing in on Gizelda and me bent over Mr. Becker.

"Hey," said Tucker when his own image appeared onscreen beside the Mombergs. Papa Momberg yelled at Karima Mansour.

"He looks pissed," I said.

"Wouldn't you be, if that was your family?"

I nodded while Tucker changed into his loafers. Then we heard voices outside. More than one. Shouting.

I tensed immediately.

"Maybe it's a patient," said Tucker, shoving the door open.

I peered over his shoulder. Call me a chicken, but I prefer to market it as "wise" and "cautious."

The doctors' lounge opened into an empty hallway. The yelling continued to our left, toward the nursing station where we'd met Rudy and Samira.

We bore left. "They could be armed," I murmured to him.

"They have metal detectors, right?"

"Security theatre," I whispered, which he understood because I'd explained it before. My ex, Ryan, had pointed out that part of security is pure show. Places have metal detectors and X-rays, but the goal is to make you *feel* safer, not because they've actually eliminated all weapons.

"You can stay in the lounge," Tucker said.

As if. I jerked my head at the people in front of the nursing station shouting in Arabic. Then I raised my eyebrows, meaning, *Do you understand anything?*

He frowned and tilted his head from side to side. *Not really.*

Greeeeeat.

"I love you," I mouthed at him.

His lips shaped it back as he squeezed my hand, but didn't break his stride.

I kept up the pace, even though every part of me screamed, *Are you nuts? Other way!*

There are security guards! Police!

Maybe the army will kick in here!

What can we do in our first half hour on-site, when we can't speak the language?

As we approached, two black-clad police officers left cubicle 5.

I sighed in relief. The police would get everything under control. Although I couldn't figure out why they headed the wrong way, even as security guards strode toward us.

Back in cubicle number 5, the patient held his bloody nose.

No. Not a patient. He still wore a white coat, his name and pathology title now spattered in blood.

I recognized the man whose broken silver glasses dangled from his left hand. It wasn't Rudy, but his quiet friend who hadn't said hello. He looked like the kind of guy who'd be good at chess or could be trusted to dog sit.

Samira, the medical student who'd directed us to the doctors' lounge, handed the pathology resident some gauze. He pressed it to his nose and fingered his swollen left cheek.

"What happened to him?" I whispered to a woman at the back of the crowd. She wore a red head scarf with a cheerful paisley pattern.

"His nose is broken," she said in English. "His jaw may be fractured also."

"But ... how did that happen?"

She shook her head and picked up a file from the nursing station instead of answering.

Someone must've seen this. It was 8:25 a.m. We'd left him and Rudy less than ten minutes ago. What about the secretary at the nursing station? A nurse or passing phlebotomist?

Tucker questioned people at the back of the crowd, but I could read their head shakes and pursed lips.

Fine. I turned my attention to the victim, standing two feet away from everyone circled around him.

"Do you need help?" I asked the pathology resident.

He shook his head and gazed over my right shoulder in a fixed way that made me turn around.

"Oh, you are the new doctors!" a skinny, bearded, 40-something man called to Tucker in a carrying tenor. "Canada, right? You must meet the chief and program director and get your paperwork in order. I will find someone to help you. Come with me."

The word *Canada* rippled through the crowd.

"Where do you come from in Canada? How did you choose our hospital?" The skinny doc, whose white coat said *Emergency Medicine*, forced a mini-smile and waved us away from cubicle number 5. I couldn't tear my eyes away from his arachnid build. His dress pants reminded me of pipe cleaners.

"Dr. Hope Sze and I are both from Montreal," said Tucker, stopping to wave me up between them.

I chose Tucker's right side instead. Can't break up the bromance.

The man frowned before he turned to me. "I am so sorry. You're from Canada also?"

My smile turned into teeth. "Born and bred."

"I see. The Chinese diaspora stretches everywhere, doesn't it?" He turned back to Tucker. "I think you'll enjoy it here very much."

My mouth hung slightly open. I reminded myself to close it.

"Dr. Sze is as Canadian as I am," said Tucker, pulling back from Dr. Arachnid to fall in step with me.

I had to smile. Tucker is a white anglophone male. He could stick with his bros and beer. Instead he chose me and a life of DEFCON 1.

"I see." Dr. Arachnid sniffed and ushered us into an elevator. He maintained a pointed silence until the doors opened, when he pointed us down a hallway on the second floor and wished us a good day.

Tucker and I stared at each other before we knocked on the closed door with a plaque that said Dr. Mostafa Sharif, Chief of Emergency Medicine.

No one answered.

I raised my eyebrows at Tucker.

Dr. Arachnid had ported us on a wild chief chase to distance us from the ruckus in the ER, where someone had hit the pathology resident.

Egypt looked so beautiful, with its real and fake palm trees, the hospital's impressive entrance, and everyone's meticulous clothes.

Yet I remembered Ryan quoting Isaac Asimov: "the rotten tree-trunk, until the very moment when the storm-blast breaks it in two, has all the appearance of might it ever had."

6

After a day of paperwork, orientation modules, and a no-show from the chief because he was apparently double-booked, we clocked out without seeing a single patient.

"What a waste," I muttered to Tucker once we stepped out into the rain. "We should've gone to the Pyramids, or King Tut, or who's the other guy—"

"Nedjemankh. You've heard of ankhs, right? Like a cross with a loop on top? Only he was called Ned-jem-ankh. I remember it like Ned doing a jam with an ankh. His coffin's not coming back 'til next week, though." Tucker checked his watch. "Want to go see the Beckers? And maybe the Mombergs?"

"Yeah, I'd like to do one clinical thing today. How's the dad's eye?"

"They're not sure yet. He had an ultrasound today."

I made a face. No one talks about the uncertainty in medicine. It's not all code blues and 16-hour transplant surgeries. Much of it involves educated guesses and watchful waiting.

Tucker adjusted his hood to shield himself from the rain. "Did Ms. Becker update you on her dad's injuries?"

"Not much. She didn't know much except that he was tubed and going to surgery. It sounded like an epidural and cerebral contusion last night, but I wonder about a subdural in an older guy. And what if the contusion was an intracranial hemorrhage?"

Tucker gave a low whistle. "Epidural, subdural, and intracranial hemorrhage. Could be all three. The trifecta. Or maybe it would be a quadrifecta? Because of the nail? I should look that up."

His phone dinged. He texted while I tried not to grind my teeth. Tooth enamel is precious. Finally, I said, "Let's go to KMT Hospital. And who are you texting?"

Tucker winked and finished his message while shielding his phone from the rain. Neither of us had brought a dry bag, since we'd expected a desert. "It's a surprise."

"Why?" Ryan never kept secrets from me. Not that I was comparing.

"Because that's the definition of the word 'surprise.' Do you feel okay taking the bus?"

I sighed. "It's like getting back on a horse, right?"

"Egggg-xactly!"

I breathed in and out, holding it for four seconds between inhalations and exhalations. It's called a box breath. Good for relaxation. 'Course I still felt more like boxing Tucker's ears as he diddled with his phone all the way to the bus stop.

"Quadfecta!" He waved his phone at me.

"Huh?"

"You know how we said trifecta, but he might have four neuro problems? In horse racing, you can also win a quadfecta, perfecta, a grand slam, a quadrella, or quaddie. They're not all the same thing. You want to hear the difference?"

I shook my head both at Tucker and the cars clogging the roads. They moved so slowly that two male drivers waved and chatted through their open windows.

"Maybe we should walk. Google says it's only another hour. Two hours, one hour, what's the diff?" I half-joked.

"We have to walk to El-Zahraa to catch the M1 anyway," said Tucker. "It'll take us 23 minutes, and we should be able to pick up something to eat on the way home."

I sighed. A normal person would head back to our hotel instead of hoofing it through the exhaust fumes.

"Or wait! We could take a taxi service down the Nile."

I perked up. "That sounds like fun. Expensive but fun."

"Hang on, I think they travel on the half hour. We're not close to one of their stops. Plus it takes an extra half hour."

I shook my head and yawned. "Not today."

"Satan?" Tucker leaned forward and pressed his forehead against mine.

I laughed and waved him away as I finished yawning. "You're more like, "Today, Satan!"

He winked at me. "Today. Tonight. Tomorrow. The ensuing fortnight ... "

Well, with that kind of attitude, he wouldn't be banging anyone else up and down the Nile. I kissed him to remind him that I was better than his text-mate.

He kissed me back so hard, my lips swelled with the pressure, and I could taste the peppermint on his tongue.

I broke off, grinning, before he pushed me against a palm tree. "Isabelle wants us to take time to sight-see. And the chief doesn't seem to care. What do you think, Tucker?"

He took a second to downshift and change gears. He shook his head. "Do you need time to recoup?"

"I don't know. I don't really stop. I just kind of keep chugging along until I fall over."

He finger-combed my hair, getting his fingers tangled, which made him laugh. "That doesn't sound good."

"Naw. You know what does, though?"

"Tell me."

I waited until we crossed a street, keeping all my senses alert to avoid getting nailed by a white truck. It still splashed us with rainwater. "First let's talk about the IED. I looked it up. The BBC said 17 people were injured."

Tucker nodded. "I saw 'at least 14,' but I'm not surprised it went up. Hope it stops there."

I ignored the use of my name as a verb, even though I subtract additional points for using it in conjunction with IED's. "Me too. I've got to tell you something before we see Mr. Becker, though."

His eyes gleamed, and he squeezed my hand. Tucker adores secrets. *"Tell* me."

"It might be nothing, but at the site, Mr. Becker apparently said something about treasure in Afrikaans."

Tucker brightened. Even his soggy bangs seemed to perk up. "What do you mean?"

"I don't know. His daughter dismissed it right after she translated it. It could've been altered mental status. He did lose consciousness a few minutes later."

"Or maybe he really hid some treasure!" Tucker whispered in my ear, sweeping me into a dance. "Calloo-callay!"

"What are you doing!"

"Waltzing in celebration. *One*-two-three, *one*-two-three."

"What the fuck is that?" I hissed, while an elderly lady shielded herself from us with her bag of groceries.

Tucker laughed before he spun me in an awkward twirl. "That's the spirit. Okay, okay."

I burst out laughing. The dude always makes me laugh. Then I detached myself before we hurt anyone, or slipped on the wet sidewalk. First walking like Egyptians, now waltzing like doofuses. "We should practice in private before we try dancing in the streets of Cairo."

Tucker flexed his arms at the elbows and wrists, pointed his hands away from his body and twitched his head from side to side.

"OMG. Are you trying the Egyptian walk again? Or vogueing?"

In response, Tucker planted his hands on his hips, pouted, and jerked his head back and forth in a pigeon-like, vaguely familiar way.

"Uh, Tucker?"

Some girls filmed him, so he kept it up for a few more seconds before he waved and blew them a kiss, sending them off in fits of giggles.

Meanwhile, I heard a meow coming from the overhang of a stone building with Roman columns and archways that had unfortunately been converted into a KFC.

Under this shelter lurked the most beautiful cat I'd ever seen, the black and orange markings on its flanks contrasting with a white body and a black mask over its kittenish face.

"Look! Our first Egyptian cat!" I pointed, charmed.

Tucker tossed his arm around me, still smiling. "Gorgeous." He pressed a kiss on my cheek. "I was channelling Mick Jagger and 'Dancing in the Street.' Do you not know any pop culture?"

"Um, no. Not if it's not on the MCAT or USMLE." Those are the Canadian medical entrance and American licensing exams. I waved at the cat. It stared at me with bright green eyes.

He sighed. "I can YouTube it for you. Well, at least you got some tips on treasure."

"Right. I wondered if you'd forgotten."

"Never. That's why I was dancing in the first place. Did Ms. Becker tell you anything else?"

"No." I pondered while the cat curled its tail into a question mark. "Well, she mentioned Johannesburg."

"Right. The South African connection. The Momberg family is from Durban. Almost the whole bus came from ZA." I figured out that was the short form for South Africa while Tucker smiled at the cat and asked, "Anything else?"

"Something about a mongoose? I know that sounds random. Oh, and he said Kruger. It reminded me of Kruger National Park." I'd always wanted to go on safari. Someday. When I was done with school and had made some inroads on my debt. In other words, in 2000 years.

Tucker snapped his fingers. "Hope, that's it! Holy—"

"What?"

"Paul Kruger!" He popped up and down on his toes and ripped his phone out of his pocket.

The cat swished its tail, watching him.

"I assume they named the park after him?"

"Yes! Stephanus Johannes Paulus Kruger. Rich dude thanks to all the coal and gold in South Africa. President of their republic. Led the Second Boer War against the British."

I peered over his shoulder. "I don't know any South African history, besides apartheid, but it says that guy died in 1904. Phillip Becker wouldn't even have been born."

"But wait! There's more." Tucker clicked on a new page with this prominent headline: **Kruger Millions**

"Are you serious?"

Tucker shook his phone at me.

I grabbed it so I could read properly. Some believe that Paul Kruger hid a cache of gold. The mythical Kruger millions, now totalling $500,000,000's worth of gold bars and coins.

I gasped.

The cat hissed back at me while Tucker laughed, and in my head, I heard the Austin Powers bad guy yelling, "Five hundred *miiiillion* dollars!"

"So the Kruger—"

Tucker touched his index finger to his lips.

I glanced from side to side. No other pedestrian appeared to be listening through the patter of raindrops, and the cat couldn't speak.

Still, I lowered my voice and handed the phone back to him. "You think *this* is related to Mr. Becker? The most likely explanation is, the stash is a myth, and Phillip Becker ended up in the wrong place at the wrong time."

"That's the most likely explanation," Tucker agreed. "And yet, it's not the most *interesting* explanation. We came here for adventure, Hope."

We stared at each other. His brown eyes gleamed back at me as the evening sun peeked from behind a cloud.

Finally, I said, "I don't like this kind of adventure. I'd rather play with unvaccinated cats. Did anyone claim responsibility for the IED?"

"No. The BBC reported on it, but they didn't say who was responsible."

"Strange, right?" As far as I know, terrorists usually can't wait to claim responsibility. A few of them can end up vying for credit.

Who would blow up a bus and fail to brag about it? And why?

"Doesn't mean it has anything to do with that." I waved my hand at his phone, my stand-in for the Kruger Millions.

Tucker nodded seriously. "Of course not."

Still, neither of us spoke as we caught the M1, which turned out to be the Cairo Metro's Line 1, and started bumping our way toward KMT hospital to visit Phillip and Gizelda Becker and the Mombergs.

"Why's it called KMT hospital, anyway?" I asked Tucker.

"It has something to do with Egypt. Hang on."

We both flipped through our phones, but I found the Wikipedia article first. "Oh, it's the ancient name for Egypt, km.t, which means black land, because the Nile would flood the riverbanks, fertilizing the land before it receded."

"Yeah. Did you see the hieroglyphs?" Tucker showed me a cute one that included a bird. "The modern name for Egypt is *Miṣr*."

"Cool." I didn't want to get Tucker's blood pressure up by pointing out the coincidence that KMT Hospital starts with the same letters as Kruger Millions.

7

"Becker?" said the KMT hospital's front desk clerk, a lovely woman with shiny, black hair down to her elbows, although her prominent incisors and darting eyes made me think of a rabbit misplaced behind a ward desk.

"Yes." I glanced at the time on my phone. The security guards had X-rayed our back packs and waved us through the metal detector, but Gizelda Becker still hadn't answered my latest texts.

Tucker drew a half-circle on my back in a wordless gesture that I knew meant *calmamente.*

I shook him off. Who wants to be calm?

The clerk frowned and clicked a few keyboard buttons before she scrolled down the screen. "Are you certain that's the name?"

"Yes, of course. Phillip Becker. KMT Hospital."

I didn't detect any Kruger Millions at KMT Hospital. The fluorescent lights flickered, and a fly landed on the desk counter in all its fuzzy black-bodied glory.

I tried not to recoil. I've occasionally seen flies buzz around Canadian hospitals. And dirty windows and peeling paint abound at St. Joe's, too. Excellent staff keep working despite pathetic surroundings.

Definite step down from the Cairo International Hospital's grand foyer, though.

I attempted to smile while displaying all of my teeth. The intensive care units are closed systems. You need a code to get in. We couldn't barge into the ICU with the security guards on standby. Time to play Ms. Nice Girl. "Look. Let me call his daughter, okay? She's expecting us."

The clerk flushed. She looked young and new and very uncomfortable. "Ma'am."

I hate people calling me ma'am. I'm not married yet. I started dialling.

"Please. Ma'am!"

Her voice caught my ear. I hung up before Ms. Becker could answer.

The clerk gazed at me with large, liquid—teary?—eyes. "I'm sorry, ma'am."

"What are you talking about?"

"He's—not there."

"What?" It was my turn to verify. "Phillip Becker, 87 years old, the father of Gizelda Becker?"

"In the ICU. Yes."

I paused. Her voice shook, and I understood why she didn't want us barging into the unit. Phillip Becker had died.

Really? Why hadn't Gizelda called me?

I cursed myself for my self-centred thinking. Gizelda Becker's father had died from an IED. Her top priority wasn't alerting me or Tucker.

"Oh. Thanks for warning me."

Tucker took my hand. "Yes, it was very kind of you. We appreciate it."

We stood beside the desk, trying to figure out what to do next. A security guard, stationed by the entrance maybe fifty feet away, watched both of us.

I swallowed hard. My animosity crumbled into fatigue. "I better text her again. To let her know we're here, if she's willing to see us."

Tucker nodded and pressed his arm unobtrusively against mine as I messaged her.

I shook my head. "I want to give her our condolences, but she could be in the ICU, or on the floor, or even back in her hotel. I mean, we don't even know when he died."

"We can try to find out," said Tucker softly.

My shoulders sagged. Jet lag. Shock. Despair. Whatever you called it, it was kicking me in the teeth. "I texted her around 2 that I was coming, and she said okay. So I think he was alive then."

"Great. And it's 7:27 now, so we've got a timeline."

Crazy how Tucker felt optimistic about a 5.5 hour time gap. I shook my head. "I know you want to see the Mombergs. Maybe we should split up."

Tucker circled his arm around me, and I felt him taking in the dusty computers and dirty floors. "Let's stick together. We'll see the Mombergs later."

"Good." The word slipped out of my throat, and Tucker grinned at me even as I said, "I don't like any of this. The IED. Mr. Becker. The Mombergs. What are we even doing in Egypt?"

"We're doing an elective and travelling the world."

"Yes, but why did they invite us? We're nobodies."

"Well, one of us is famous." Tucker winked at me, using his closest eye since we were already sandwiched hip to hip, still under the guards' watchful gaze.

I sighed. You'd think no one would pay attention to a resident doctor from a country best known for hockey and Tim Hortons, but as my little brother Kevin pointed out, my side gig of crime-busting has acquired a small cult following. Kevin's reported fake Facebook, Twitter, and Instagram accounts masquerading as me, but he can't stop memes, Pinterest boards of photos and articles, or "fan" accounts like @detectivedocterz.

"You've got hits as far away as the Middle East, Tokyo, and even one in Antarctica," Kevin told me a week ago.

"Antarctica? That one's *got* to be fake news."

Kevin shrugged. "Why? They're as bored as everyone else. Maybe more."

"Thanks a lot!" I started to punch his shoulder, remembered that he was cleaning up my online act for free, and stopped in mid-air.

"I'm telling you, Hope, your fans want to hear from you. You better start using social media, or everyone else is gonna do it for you."

Kevin was angling for me to hire him as a social media consultant. But he was right, my followers could have played a role in Sarquet Industries' recruitment process. Once everything calmed down, I vowed to meet Isabelle face to face and shake the truth out of her.

In the meantime, I ignored my D class Internet fame. George Takei pointed out, "Social media is like ancient Egypt: writing things on walls and worshiping cats." If my nine-year-old little brother could cover it, I wouldn't get too excited about it.

"While we're waiting for Gizelda, we could grab a bite to eat," said Tucker.

My stomach was gnawing on its own lining, but it seemed disrespectful to chow down right after Mr. Becker had died. I shook my head.

"Okay," said Tucker, "let's buy her flowers. We can leave them in his room, even if she doesn't want to talk to us."

"Good idea. We just need to make sure that she's still here. Otherwise, we need to figure out where she's staying."

The desk clerk helped us out by calling up to the ICU. Yes, Ms. Becker was clearing out her father's things, but still in the building.

So we swooped down to the gift shop, with me trying not to wince at the price of a slightly wilted bouquet of yellow roses.

"The money will go to the hospital," said Tucker. He added under his breath, gazing at the dirty tile floor, "They need it."

In the elevator up to the third floor ICU, Tucker watched me check my phone and come up empty. "Don't worry about it. Like I said, we'll leave the roses at the nursing station if we have to. What's the worst that can happen? We'll brighten their day."

He waved the flowers at me until I laughed and took them, cradling them in my arms like a baby.

Soon we faced the frosted, locked ICU doors. Tucker hit the speaker on the right and spoke to the nurse about Ms. Becker.

"Oh," piped a female nurse, "she's meeting a friend in our waiting area. The code is 27379 if you want to come in and say hello."

Tucker plugged in the numbers in the keypad on the wall. The doors slid open automatically.

I glanced to the left and saw a water cooler outside the public bathrooms. Good news, since you can't drink the tap water in Egypt, and it was stressing me out to buy bottled water and dispose of single use plastics.

"Here's the waiting room." Tucker pointed to an alcove to our right with chairs lined along three sides.

The room was small but freshly painted, with a bookshelf on the left wall and a TV mounted in the corner. Even though night had fallen, I appreciated how the windows let the street light in to help illuminate a print of irises on the right wall.

No sign of Ms. Becker, though. I frowned at the silent phone in my free hand.

I turned to Tucker. "Do you think we just missed her?"

"It's possible," he said slowly, right before the women's bathroom door opposite us swung open.

Out stepped a bespectacled man in a suit with short-cropped curly black hair, olive skin, and a slightly bulbous nose. A guy coming out of the woman's bathroom would've startled me enough in a Muslim country, but I recognized the woman following on his heels, a senior citizen with a chignon of greying brown hair.

My mouth fell open. "Ms. Becker?"

8

G izelda Becker gasped and took a step backwards, her bum bumping the bathroom door inward.

The man, who was a step ahead of her, threw his arms out as if to shield her.

The movement drew his black suit jacket open, and I gawked at the familiar black cobra fanny pack clipped to his waist.

I pointed at the bag. "Hey. Isn't that—"

The man swept his jacket closed and tried to button it over the fanny pack as he headed out the frosted doors. "All will be well, Ms. Becker. Good evening. Peace be with you."

Where the heck was he going? I turned to Gizelda and thrust the roses at her. "I'm so sorry about your father."

She automatically accepted the bouquet, even though her mouth still gaped open.

"I'll be back in a second, after I talk to your—friend." The frosted doors sealed behind him.

I could feel Tucker's confusion, but I didn't have time to explain beyond an urgent look.

How many men wear any sort of fanny pack, let alone one emblazoned with a cobra?

Even an IED couldn't erase it from my memory. I'd unbuckled it from around Mr. Becker's waist, and within hours of his death, his daughter had handed that cobra bag over to a stranger.

I needed to know why.

"No. No!" Gizelda cried behind me.

"It's okay, Tucker will help you with the flowers," I called over my shoulder as I slipped into the hallway and followed that man. His soles echoed off the tile floor in the otherwise empty corridor.

"Hello!"

He didn't turn around, but his head twitched to listen to my sneakers thumping behind him.

"Sir, I'm Dr. Hope Sze."

He couldn't run, or didn't want to run, in black leather dress shoes, but he stepped up the pace.

"I just have a few questions."

He turned for the elevator at the end of the hall.

I broke into a run. "It'll only take a few minutes! Please."

He punched the elevator button repeatedly, but I knew that wouldn't net him a fast getaway in a decrepit hospital.

"Marhaba!" I called, closing in. Cobra Guy had spoken good English to Ms. Becker, but I might as well try out my fledgling Arabic, even if I reminded myself of white people screaming *"Ni hao!"* at me across the street.

At 5'2" and a quarter, no one considers me physically intimidating. Even my little bro is gaining on me. But Cobra Guy's eyes widened in fear before he broke for the stairs across from the elevator.

"No, I just want to talk to you. Please!"

"Hope!" Tucker thundered behind me.

"Can't talk. Running!" I shouted as I shoved open the stair door and rushed down each step. Good thing we were only on the third floor.

"Hope! *Afwan!*"

If anything, Tucker's Arabic ratcheted Cobra Guy up to sprint mode.

"Stay with her!" I howled at Tucker, and gunned it.

I heard the third floor door swing open above me. Tucker had ignored me and abandoned Gizelda, but I couldn't waste the breath to tell him off.

Still, irritation meant I fell a few crucial seconds behind. Yeah, must've been that, and not me being less fit than a thirtyish guy in a suit.

I banged open the stair door on the first floor and pelted after him, shocked at the number of people crowding the lobby. Did KMT have a second stage of visiting hours? How many family members hung out in a hospital at dinner time?

Cobra Guy darted around a family of six. The mother cried out and yanked a toddler up to her chest. The father berated Cobra Guy but made no move to stop him.

"Excuse me!" I called.

The family clustered together in the middle of the hall, still focused on the guy, three kids wailing, one dad cursing, all of them blocking my way.

"Marhaba! Shokran! Please, I want to talk to him!" I wove around them, side-stepping a stroller and multiple small shoes.

Another guy glanced up from his cell phone before he walk-texted directly into my path.

"It's important!" I snapped, edging against the wall to sneak around him. Cobra Guy had nearly reached the security guards.

"Hope!" Tucker bellowed behind me.

"He's getting away, Tucker!"

"Do you need help?" asked an older man with an impressive beard.

"Yes, I want to talk to the man in the suit. Please!"

Beard Man frowned and surveyed the crowd, meditating on my words.

I lowered my voice. "It's about my friend who passed away."

Beard Man raised his hands in the air and issued a short speech.

The crowd chattered amongst themselves, but slowly, reluctantly, they parted toward the edges of the hallway.

Moses parted the Red Sea; Beard Man parted the hospital horde.

"Thank you so much, sir. Much appreciated. Excuse me! Thank you."

Tucker caught up with me, and I huffed, "I swear I'm not crazy."

"I trust you," he said. That's exactly why I love him.

We dashed down the hall, which ended in a three-way juncture, one of which exited to the outside.

I gambled on the exit and rushed through the outer doors. "Hello! Sir. Please!"

A white checker-boarded taxi squealed away from the curb with Cobra Guy barely visible in the passenger seat.

9

B ack upstairs, we discovered Gizelda Becker deep in conversation with another man.

What the heck? Did she have an unending supply of men? This one was twice the age of Cobra Guy, though.

I surveyed the deeply-tanned, salt-and-pepper-haired, barrel-shaped man, who looked like an ex football player plus four decades, shoehorned into a suit. I couldn't make out his eyes behind tinted glasses. Then I recognized that narrow Becker nose.

I slowed down. Tucker tugged my hand, hauling me forward and waving at them.

The guy glanced up, frowning. Gizelda wheeled toward us, waving the roses in her left hand.

I stopped short, assessing the faint resemblance between this man and Gizelda, in addition to the noses. Maybe it was the way they stood, their shoulders hunched together. Maybe it was their chins. Even though he was taller and stockier than her, something about them matched.

"Dr. Tucker. Dr. Sze," she said, pointing at us with her bouquet.

"These are ... our father's doctors?" said the man, with the same accent. He frowned harder, probably because we looked too young and foreign, but he held out his hand to Tucker.

Tucker turned to me.

The man belatedly decided to shake hands with me first and pivoted with his hand still extended. His grip was warm and slightly rough, but he didn't squeeze my hand too hard, and his cologne didn't make me hold my breath, so I nodded and tried to smile. "Please accept our condolences. We offered your father pre-hospital care. Hi, I'm Dr. Hope Sze."

Tucker took the man's hand next. "I'm so sorry for your loss. Please call me Tucker, short for Dr. John Tucker. We're Canadian resident doctors visiting Egypt."

"Thank you." The man grimaced and rubbed his left cheek. "Our poor father. We appreciate all you've done. My name is Luke Becker. Phillip's son. Gizelda's brother."

"Oh. I didn't see you on the bus. Did I miss you?" I glanced at his sister, but she'd pulled out her phone, thumbing through her texts as she held the flowers with her other hand.

"I was in Johannesburg. I grabbed the first flight as soon as I heard about my father and the IED. I just arrived from the airport."

"I'm so sorry," I said to both of them.

Gizelda nodded briefly before fixing back on her phone.

Luke pressed his lips together and adjusted what might have been a Rolex before touching his navy tie, drawing attention to his well-cut charcoal suit, gleaming black leather shoes, and gold wedding band.

Meanwhile, I felt like hospital germs pranced across my skin. We'd changed but hadn't showered after leaving our hospital to come to KMT.

"Gizelda," said Luke.

She wrenched her head up, eyes widening as if she'd already forgotten us.

Luke patted her shoulder. "Why don't you thank the doctors for their help and let them get on with their night."

"Of course! Not only did you help, you gave me these roses. You must think me a mannerless boor." She tucked her phone in her purse. Her knuckles shone white as she clutched the roses with her other hand.

"I think you're grieving," I said quietly.

A laugh jerked out of her mouth. "Yes. I am."

"Are you okay?" I kept my eyes on her instead of Luke, whom I could see flexing his fingers out of the corners of my eyes. Tucker shifted his weight from foot to foot.

"Yes. All right. I'm trying to process ... our mother and now our father."

"Oh, no. What happened to your mother?" I said.

Luke cleared his throat.

"If it's too painful—" said Tucker.

"She also ... died suddenly." Gizelda covered her mouth, inhaling and exhaling slowly over the roses before she could speak again. "It brings back bad memories."

"How awful." We often write "died suddenly" in an obituary to describe a suicide. I winced in sympathy.

Tucker said, "A loss on top of a loss is very difficult. We're so sorry to hear that."

"We'll work it out. It's very sad, but we lost her in 2017," said Luke. "We've had a few years to adjust. Other people have dealt with worse."

"That's true." Gizelda's eyes filled with tears, and the roses wobbled in the air as she reached into her purse for a tissue.

Luke threw his arm around her and squeezed her shoulders. "We made it through that. We'll make it through this, too."

She said, so low that I dipped my head to hear her, "Our poor father. Why did he have to go like this?"

"Terrorists." Luke added something I didn't understand, presumably in Afrikaans.

She nodded and blew her nose before balling the tissue in her palm. Now she had no free hands. I felt like offering to hold the roses so she wouldn't be so burdened.

Instead, I squeezed Tucker's hand and cleared my throat. "Uh. Is there anything we can do for you? Maybe get you a beverage or a hot meal?" I turned to include Luke in the invitation. "Sometimes a walk outside helps."

Gizelda peered at me for a second, almost like she was trying to decode my face, before she abruptly handed the roses back to me. The plastic made a crinkling noise. "Please. I can't accept these. They remind me too much of my mother's funeral. Our aunt sent a car made out of roses."

"Oh, no. I've never heard of a car made out of roses," I said, accepting the bouquet. The roses smelled sweet. Up close, I noticed a few more crumpled, decaying petals.

"Is that a South African tradition?" asked Tucker, whose brain contains a constantly-updated encyclopedia comparing and contrasting cultural differences.

"Not at all. It was a gesture of respect," said Luke, hugging his sister against his side. He was so big that he nearly lifted her off her feet.

"Because your mother loved cars?" I ventured. It seemed less likely that a deceased 87-year-old's wife had raced cars, but never say never. Fingers crossed that I'll zoom around as an octogenarian, plus Mrs. Phillip Becker could have been much younger than her husband.

Gizelda Becker made a strange noise somewhere between a laugh and a sob. Her brother released her as she reached for another tissue. "No. She died in one. A car accident."

Whoa. I swung the roses behind my back. "I'm so sorry."

Tucker made sympathetic noises for both of us.

She closed her eyes. "I didn't go to Luke's with my mother. I should have been driving. My father had a headache, so I stayed with him, but our mother took social commitments very seriously. She missed her grandchildren and insisted on driving herself. The autopsy—"

Luke shook his head and clapped her on her shoulder. "Don't torture yourself, Gizelda."

She squeezed her eyes shut and visibly tried to calm herself down, even though tears glistened in the seams of her eyelids. "She went through the windshield."

I started to reach for her with my rose hand, but I didn't know her well enough to make contact even if my fingers were free. "You've endured so much. I wish we could help."

"She should have worn her seat belt. And our poor, poor father. Oh, God. Why did he make us come back here?" Her knees sagged. Luke caught her.

Tucker looked agonized. He squeezed my hand so hard that it hurt.

"We'll need some time to process this," said Luke, his voice slightly hoarse.

"Of course. Please contact us if you think we can be of any help. You have our numbers, right?" said Tucker. He let me go so he could enter their contact information in his phone.

Gizelda dug more tissues out of her purse. "Father would have been safe at home. I could have protected him."

"Please don't blame yourself," I whispered.

"You can reach out to us any time," said Tucker. "Please. Day or night. We're still on Canadian time anyway. We're so sorry for your losses. We didn't mean to intrude."

Luke shook his head. "We should be fine. Thank you. I'll make arrangements for our father."

Shipping their father's remains to the other end of the continent must be an ordeal. I said, "If you need help, I could ask Sarquet Industries for advice. They're an international corporation." Not that EMR software would have much to do with funeral arrangements, but as far as I was concerned, Isabelle and Youssef owed us one.

Luke pursed his lips. "I appreciate the thought. We'll take it from here."

"Of course," I said, and Tucker and I withdrew together, me leaning forward to hide the bouquet. My stomach churned. Roses would never smell the same to me again.

I bet they wouldn't call. They'd stay locked in their grief. Selfishly, that meant I could never ask Gizelda Becker about the cobra bag, let alone the mysterious man and the Kruger millions.

10

"We really stepped in it. What are the chances that roses would make her cry?" I whispered to Tucker as we rode the elevator to visit the Momberg family on the seventh floor.

He nodded and glanced at our reflection in the fingerprint-smudged steel doors. "Bad luck. You never know what triggers anyone, especially right after a death."

"It's crazy that both their parents died 'suddenly.'"

Tucker gave a lopsided smile. "My friends tell me lots of wild stories about South Africa."

"But poor Mr. Becker died in *Egypt.*" I swung the bouquet for punctuation, yanking the roses back before they touched the elevator walls.

"Bad things can happen anywhere. You know that better than anyone."

"Totally. If people saw me at St. Joe's, they'd call Canada the world murder capital."

"That's my girl. Killer karma." Tucker tilted his head. "That's just you, though. South Africa's like its own murder ball."

I nodded. "I guess that's what happens when you build your

economy on slavery and apartheid. Thank God Nelson Mandela somehow became president."

The elevator binged in agreement. We trotted down the corridor toward the Mombergs' room while Tucker scrolled through his phone and offered South African statistics.

"Fifty-eight murders per day. Rising steadily since 2011. I guess the only upside is that there are fewer sexual assaults than from 2009 to 2015."

"Good."

"Oh, wait. Sexual assaults are on the upswing for the past three years."

"Ugh. Sounds like a war zone." I felt like plugging my ears and chanting la-la-la. I sniffed the roses to make me feel better.

"Not as bad as real war zones like Syria, Afghanistan, or Yemen—unless you cone down to specific townships like Philippi East in Cape Town. Then it's worse." Tucker clicked off his phone and dropped it in his pocket, grabbing my free hand.

"The Beckers don't look like they're from a rough township, but I guess they could be." I held up the wilted roses. "Um, you think the gift shop will give us our money back?"

Tucker snorted. "Are you kidding? You keep 'em."

"I don't need them."

"Hope! You're so cheap. Just take the roses. When we're rich, I'll shower you in roses."

I shook my head. "Roses take pesticides and growing space and water that could be used on food, not to mention the carbon footprint of flying them around the world."

He sighed. "You're right. Total buzz kill, though. Well, let's see if the Mombergs want them."

"Sure. Let's do it."

"Ho ho ho." Tucker grinned at me, and I scanned the corridor to make sure we weren't offending anyone.

A tired-looking woman in blue scrubs and no head scarf padded past us in her running shoes, dinner in hand. I thought I could smell chicken and rice, and my stomach gurgled, even though I haven't eaten meat in two months.

"I'll take you out for supper afterward. I know the perfect place. One of my buddies recommended it." He knocked on the door of room 7604. "Mr. and Mrs. Momberg?"

"Frederik and Noeline, please. Oh! You brought us roses?" Noeline's plump, bruised face, with a nasty cut on her right cheek and a few more superficial lacerations, softened as I presented her with the bouquet. She inhaled the roses' scent. 'They remind me of home. Thank you."

"It's nothing."

Their son Jaco watched with wide eyes as I shifted from foot to foot, embarrassed at the second-hand flowers. The entire family seemed to be wearing the same clothes as yesterday

The little girl, Fleur, tugged at the mom's pants, dislodging them. "Mommy okay?"

Noeline grabbed her waistband and hiked it back up above her hips before her underpants showed. "Yes, fine, of course, no problem."

Their lacerations and fatigue and Fleur's tangled hair begged to differ. I gazed past them to see Tucker shaking hands with the dad, Frederik, who sat on the side of the bed with his right eye bandaged up.

Frederik bowed his head and said, "Thank you."

"The flowers were nothing," I said, determined to change the subject.

Noeline raised her face from them. "Oh, do you know the history of roses in South Africa?"

That's one subject that has never come up in my life, but Tucker grinned. "Please tell us."

She awarded him a tremulous smile. "We consider roses one of South Africa's first settlers. Jan van Riebeeck brought rose trees from Holland and grew the first Dutch rose on November first, 1659."

Ouch. I'm sure many people lived in that territory before 1659. And I wondered how roses had affected South Africa's ecosystem, considering the "settlers'" brutal treatment of human beings.

"Ah," I said. I'd better not bring up politics when her husband could lose an eye.

Frederik raised his hand. "They don't want to hear about this, Noeline."

"Oh, we don't mind." Tucker grinned at her. "South Africa is quite famous for its roses. Isn't one of them named after Nelson Mandela?"

The little boy, Jaco, giggled and clapped his hand over his mouth before Frederik frowned at him. "It's very kind of you to stop by with flowers, but have you heard anything about my eye?"

Tucker sobered immediately. "I haven't had a chance to speak to anyone, but with your permission, I could do so."

"I give you permission. I don't care what I have to sign. I want some answers. And if you don't get any of those, I'm going straight home." He mumbled to himself in Afrikaans in such an ominous tone that his wife gasped and I glanced at the children, who watched their father, wide-eyed, as he added something about Phillip Becker.

Noeline placed a hand on her husband's, trying to calm him. "We're so sorry to hear Mr. Becker has passed. We heard his son flew up. I'm glad the brother and sister are together now. Very sad."

"Very sad. Just goes to show, you never know what's going to happen," said Tucker.

The little girl bounced up and down on her toes between her parents while Noeline filled a cardboard urinal with water to use as a makeshift vase.

"Imagine a mine owner getting hit by an IED in Egypt." Frederik laughed a little too loud.

I stared at him while the children smiled uncertainly.

Noeline turned around with a fake smile. "You'll have to excuse my husband. Sometimes he speaks without thinking."

"Did you get to know the Beckers on tour?" I asked.

She shook her head. "Not very much. They upgraded their hotels and would only join us for certain excursions."

"I wonder why they paid for the tour at all," said Frederik, beginning to pace. He obviously felt trapped in the small room with one cramped bathroom and one dirty window.

"Why? I heard him say it was safer in a group. Less of a target that way," said Noeline. "I used to talk to Gizelda a little. She liked the children. She missed her nieces and nephews."

"She's all right," said Frederik, smoothing Fleur's hair and sticking out his tongue to make her laugh.

"Did you talk to Mr. Becker, too?" I asked.

Noeline blushed and shook her head, the roses still in one hand.

"I offered him a beer once," said Frederik. "Turned me down flat. Said he had too much work to do. Work? An old man like him? He's on vacation. And what kind of work does he do, anyway? I know mine owners. They sit on their money."

"I'm sure they work *very hard,*" Noeline insisted as Jaco absorbed every word. Meanwhile, Fleur spun in circles, watching her bloodied skirt flare with every turn.

"Yeah, what the hell. He's gone now, anyway." Frederik picked up his son and tossed him a few inches in the air, making him laugh before he caught him again.

"My turn! My turn!" Fleur bounced up and down on her toes.

"Did you know the Beckers from before, in South Africa?" I said.

Frederik bellowed with laughter. "You hear what I said? The Becker family owns the Sacco Manganese Mines. You know how much money that is? You think they hang around with a truck driver and his family in Durban?"

"They came on tour with you," I said.

Frederik gave Fleur one, two, three tosses. He raised his voice over her giggles. "Hardly. Didn't eat any of the meals. Only came with us for the museum tours, and even then, they were gone half the time."

Jaco tugged on his father's belt loop, and Frederik set his daughter down so he could heft Jaco in the air once more. "Oof, you're getting heavy, boy."

"No, I'm not!"

"Two more. One, two!" Frederik set his son down and said, "Phillip had 'private meetings' scheduled everywhere around the city and all the museum men in his pocket. I tell you, they should have gotten a refund. The most time they spent with us was that bus ride, and look what happened."

"Frederik." This time, Noeline added something in Afrikaans.

"I'm sorry," Frederik told us, running his hand through his sweaty, receding hairline. "I shouldn't say such things. The man is dead. Sometimes I speak before I think." He bared his teeth at his children. "Don't be an old fool like your father, hey?"

Fleur laughed and pretended to snarl back at him, while Jaco looked puzzled. He could probably feel the strange undercurrents in the room.

"Did Mr. Becker ever talk about Kruger?" I asked Noeline.

"The park?" she asked, startled.

"I don't know," I admitted. "When Mr. Becker was hurt, he mentioned the word Kruger, but he was speaking in Afrikaans."

"Oh, goodness. We've brought the children to Kruger several times, and we've talked to them about how terrible it is to poach the rhino horns, but I didn't mention that to Gizelda, no."

"What did you talk about?"

She shrugged. "She asked me about the children and if I needed any help. They can be a handful. She was busy with her own father, though."

"What did she have to do for him?" Tucker asked. "Was he physically weak?"

Frederik snorted. "The man seemed all right to me. It wasn't like he couldn't order his own food and complain if the coffee wasn't hot enough."

"He had a cane, and she made sure to keep track of their bags and their personal items," said Noeline, with a warning look at Frederik. "He was always talking to her, asking her to take notes, that sort of thing."

"Take notes. About what?" I said. I couldn't imagine my father dictating at me.

"Sometimes it sounded like mine business. Usually he talked about Egyptian history. He seemed quite taken with Osiris and

Horus. I don't know. These two keep me very busy." She winked at her children.

"Yes, it was mainly that kind of historical nonsense," said Frederik. "Every other sentence, he'd say to his daughter, 'Remember that!' Or 'Mark that down!' So she did. I've worked with people like that. Easier to write it all down than to brush them off."

Man, I needed access to those notes. I'd memorize them right after quizzing her about the cobra fanny pack. Tucker and I exchanged a glance, and I knew his brain had latched back onto the Kruger millions. As my grade eight teacher used to joke, *Great minds think alike—and small minds seldom differ.*

"Did she take notes on paper, or on her phone?" I asked.

"She had a little red book!" Fleur burst out. "It was so pretty. I wanted to draw in it, remember, Ma?"

Noeline laughed. "Yes, but we don't touch other people's things, right, sweetie?"

"I do!" said Jaco, while Fleur pouted and the adults laughed.

Tucker smiled at the Mombergs. "I'm tempted to do the same myself. Did you happen to notice the black leather bag around his waist? The one with a cobra on it?"

Frederik shrugged. "I may have seen it. What about it?"

"It's an unusual bag. I wonder what was inside it?" Tucker's pale cheeks reddened while both of us pretended not to notice. *Act normal, and maybe you'll look normal.*

Frederik shrugged again. "He probably had his passport and money in it, the way all of us do."

Noeline nodded in agreement.

"You saw him taking his passport out of the cobra bag?" I asked.

Frederik shook his head. "I'm not looking at Phillip Becker."

Noeline said, "We're too busy with our little ones."

Neither of them met our gaze. I could tell from Tucker's stillness that he noticed, too.

Someone else on the bus might have seen what Mr. Becker kept inside that cobra bag. I had the number for the tour guide with the turban, Muhamed. I itched to call him.

"Well," said Noeline, in a falsely bright voice, "it must be a long day for you too."

I started to wish them a good night, but Jaco piped up. "I can tell you."

I peered at the little boy. "You know what's inside the bag?"

He shook his head. "No. I wanted to look inside, though. Because the cobra was so scary!"

"So you opened it when he wasn't looking?" I prompted him the same way I ask patients about cigarette and alcohol use: anticipating a "bad" answer so they don't have to feel as guilty admitting it.

He shook his head again, gravely. "He never opened it. He had a —" He spoke to his mother, who interpreted.

Noeline wiped chocolate off Fleur's mouth as she answered. "Mr. Becker kept his money and passport in a pouch around his thigh. Yes, now that you mention it, Jaco, I remember him using that. That's far more likely for a South African, by the way. I thought it was strange that he'd carry anything valuable in that waist pouch, where it would attract a thief's attention. My countrymen know to be more careful than that."

But why would Phillip Becker carry a fanny pack around his waist and never open it? And why was it so important that his daughter got rid of it right after he died?

I pasted a smile on my face. "You've given us lots to think about. Thanks so much for your patience."

"You must be exhausted," Noeline agreed, immediately seeing us to the door in a way that meant she wanted us out of there, roses or no roses. "You've been so kind to us. I'd like to give you something."

"No need," Tucker assured her.

"We don't have a lot. Not like some," she said, clearly meaning the Beckers. She glanced down at her children and brightened. "I know. We bought little keepsakes to give to our friends when we go home. I'd like to give you this." She unclasped her necklace and detached a small silver symbol, ♀. The cross with a loop on top. The same type I'd seen around Gizelda Becker's neck after the IED, but Noeline's ankh was much smaller and diamond-free. Now that I thought about it, my dad had once bought me ankh earrings.

I shook my head. "No, thank you. We don't need anything. We didn't do much for you."

"Speak for yourself," Tucker whispered behind me, to make me laugh, and it almost worked. My lips quirked.

"It's very small," said Noeline. "It wouldn't even cost five dollars in your currency. But you know the ankh, right? It means life. I think that's very appropriate for you and your boyfriend, as doctors. I'd like you to have it and to pray for my husband's eye."

I felt like she'd socked me in the stomach. "I'm sorry. I can send good wishes, but I'm not religious."

"Take it anyway. Please. And I'd like to share the roses with you, too. I consider them a bond between us. I want to believe that Frederik will see again."

Yikes. No way to turn her down now. "I want to believe that, too."

"Then it's settled." She sent us on our way with the ankh and four roses. "One for each of you, and two more to grow on." She winked in a way that included her two children, implying that Tucker and I would procreate soon.

I ended up red-faced, holding the ankh and the roses, and secretly wishing I could tell her that four is a bad luck number in Chinese.

11

I zipped the ankh into a compartment of my own thigh pouch before we finally escaped the hospital in search of food. Tucker urged me into a 20-person lineup outside a small restaurant five blocks away. "Want some shawarma? This one is supposed to be the best."

The smell of grilled meat and deep-fried food evaporated my fatigue and my embarrassment over the roses. "Hell, yeah."

Tucker pointed at the Coca-Cola machine behind the counter. "Everyone on TripTalk recommends the fresh mango juice."

"Awesome. You think they have vegetarian options?" I've avoided meat since our hostage taking on November fourteenth, which I call 14/11.

"I'll ask." Tucker squinted at the menu in Arabic.

"Make sure you order at least three. They are very small, like sliders," said a guy in front of us. He looked our age, late twenties, with a long chin and a New York Yankees baseball cap pulled low on his head.

"I eat ten!" said a rotund fifty-ish woman behind us, patting her belly.

The Yankees guy nodded. "Sometimes I do, too."

I laughed, and for the first time, I felt myself relax. Ten sliders! Bring it home!

"These are the best shawarma in Cairo," the Yankees guy told us.

The woman wouldn't let him outdo her. "Best in Egypt! When my friends visit, I take them straight here. I've been coming here for 26 years. One of them swore she would only ever eat Syrian and Turkish shawarma because they were superior, and now she wishes I could send her one in the mail. And to answer your question about meat, you may have Egyptian roumy cheese or sujuk sausage instead of beef, if you prefer. It will taste as good as your roses are beautiful."

Tucker raised his eyebrows, gazed at my flowers, and back at the woman.

I instantly bestowed the roses upon her.

She burst out laughing. "Oh, you keep them instead of giving them to a nosy, old woman."

"You're not old, and it's a long way back to our hotel," I said. I'd rather award the flowers to a cheerful woman instead of keeping them as a reminder of our 0 for 2 hospital visits.

"Very well, then. You must let me take a picture of you and post it on my Instagram to thank you."

I made a face. "Why don't we just take a picture of you?"

"No, please! I would love to have more young people on my Insta!"

I burst out laughing, and somehow she roped me, Tucker, the Yankees guy, and his friends, plus her and her roses, into a picture. Actually, five pictures, because it was impossible for all of us to look good at the same time.

"There. I am Maryam al-Banhawi, and we are all friends now."

"Maryam," I repeated, because it was easier than al-Banhawi. I only had to remember not to say Miriam by accident. She and Tucker exchanged Instagram handles and followed each other.

Maryam scrolled through his newsfeed. "Ah, yes. Very nice. Such a beautiful young couple, and you're doctors, too. Your family must be so proud!"

"We still have more training to do," I explained, but she waved it away and said, "I would like to treat you to dinner. Whatever you like. It's on the house."

"No, it's okay, Maryam."

"I insist. You give me roses, I buy you dinner. I try to repay generosity with generosity. Do you know the New Testament?"

My smile ossified slightly. "I'm agnostic."

She thumped her own chest. "I'm a good Christian. Did you know that 10 percent of Egyptians are Coptic Christians? 'And he said unto them, Take heed, and beware of covetousness: for a man's life consisteth not in the abundance of the things which he possesseth.' Luke 12:15."

Now I felt decidedly weird about her generosity. I covet things all the time, especially food. "Uh, Maryam, please—"

Tucker protested in Arabic, and the Yankees guy pleaded our case, but by the time we got to the front of the line and Tucker opened his mouth, she'd already ordered ten beef, three sausage, and seven roumy shawarmas for us. "With one mango juice and one pomegranate juice. And extra spicy pickles!"

When we tried to pay, Maryam literally pushed our cards away with her rose-free hand and berated the clerk into taking her credit card. "You are our guests. Tell your friends how much fun you're having in Egypt, @DrJohnTucker!"

Tucker and I walked into the night, stuffing our faces as tahini and juice dripped down our arms.

"This is fantastic," I raved, between bites.

"Tell me about it," Tucker ground out. Usually he doesn't eat as fast as me, but this time he was matching me shawarma for shawarma.

Maryam had even managed to order different types of buns. Although I've never considered pita bread more than a blank canvas, this one was nice and fresh, and I loved the buttery kaiser buns that contrasted with the sharp tang of roumy cheese.

Every time I needed to wake up my palate, I'd choose either soothing mango juice or the slightly tart pomegranate.

"I have to have more," said Tucker, once we were only left with wrappers. "I could go there for 26 years."

"And bring your friends," I agreed, sucking up the very last of the mango juice.

I thought of our friend Tori Yamamoto, who had made us a card before our flight. She drew a picture of a woman in silhouette on the front, and inside, she wrote, *"Night came walking through Egypt swishing her black dress."~Zora Neale Hurston*

I swished through the Egyptian night with the man I loved, my tongue full of new flavours, my belly finally full.

I also loved the quote Tori had added on the back, from Naguib Mahfouz, whom she said was an Egyptian writer and the only Arab writer to have won the Nobel Prize. *"Fear does not prevent death, it prevents life."*

Back at the hotel, I could have hit the bed immediately, my brain reeling with unexpected friendship.

Instead, I took a quick shower with Tucker (heh heh heh), slid my feet into those terry cloth slippers, and set up my laptop at the desk to learn more about Mr. Phillip Becker. Although it was a fairly common name, I was able to narrow him down by his country and a daughter named Gizelda.

Phillip's father, Roelof "Pik" Becker, launched the Sacco Manganese Mines in 1928. I assumed they called him "Pik" after a pickaxe, what with the mining and all, but no. Pik's friends called him *pikkewyn*, which is Afrikaans for penguin, because Pik liked to wear dark suits or dinner jackets.

I showed Tucker the picture of Pik at a *braai*, or barbecue, all suited up.

He grinned from the bed, where he sat with his tablet. "Yeah, I saw that Pik was a mining engineer who emigrated to South Africa in 1926. Crazy."

I nodded. "I wonder how much money he made off the Kalahari manganese field?"

"Enough to send Phillip to private school in the KwaZulu-Natal midlands and geology at the University of Witwatersrand." He relished pronouncing the names. Then he patted the bed, encouraging me to crawl next to him.

I did, enjoying the feeling of the sheets against my skin before I curled up next to his warm body and brought up my knees to use as a shelf for my laptop. "Phillip was kind of a jock in his day, eh? Sounds like he was all-star at cricket and hockey back then. They called him the Meerkat."

"Yeah, he was still in good shape even 20 years ago. He won the world championship in squash for his age."

"Hmmm." There's a big difference between 67 and 87, but Phillip Becker sounded like he'd been in relatively excellent shape, aside from emphysema. "Did you see the article on Phillip's mineral collection?"

Tucker's teeth gleamed in the glow from his computer screen. "I've been admiring photos of Tsumeb schneiderhöhnite and a malachite sphere."

"Pretty," I said, although one of the rocks looked like a black yam with green asparagus minerals growing out the top, and the malachite sphere made me think of something an alien might snack on. "Check this out. He owned an 'exceptional, world class collection of minerals from Southern Africa.' He basically had a museum in his basement."

"Right, he built a display for 3400 specimens, some of them viewable from 360 degrees, in a dust-free environment, with professional lighting and ventilation, in 2018." Tucker whistled. "The guy is *loaded.* I mean, was loaded. Where are you going with this?"

"Well, two things. They say that some of those minerals come from the Kalahari manganese field that Phillip would've accessed through his dad, but they also mention Mozambique, the Congo, Russia, Morocco, China, and Pakistan. Ten to one, he would have hunted for rocks in Egypt."

"Sure. Gizelda or her brother mentioned he'd been here before, right?"

"Yeah." The despair in Gizelda's voice had seared itself into my brain. *Oh, God. Why did he make us come back here?* "If he was in such good shape, why did he need his daughter? Why sign them up for a tour he barely used?"

"Does seem weird. He could've just gone to the museums he wanted and flown home again instead of waiting for the group schedule."

"Right. I don't know if Egypt has a big mining industry, but it deals a lot in antiquities and collectibles. I bet that even if he wasn't after a stone specifically from Egypt, someone here could have hooked him up. Remember Frederik Momberg said Phillip was friends with all the museum curators?"

Tucker bent over me and licked the upper curve of my ear. "I'll be your friend and curate every part of you."

I squealed. My ears are ticklish. "Hang on." I scrolled up to the first photo. "This is Phillip Becker and his wife Rosetta with that all-star mineral collection. They mention Gizelda and her brother—looks like his real name is Luca. Gizelda's divorced, but Luca and his wife had five children."

Tucker's hands passed over my breasts in a way that made it clear he was more interested in activities that made children than in contemplation of other people's progeny. "What about them?"

"Well—" I grabbed his hands and planted them on his own main event—"you're convinced it's the Kruger millions, but the Beckers have plenty of their own treasure. They were rich. And you know that when someone dies under strange circumstances, you should always follow the money. I know it's an IED. I know we're not following the rules. But somehow, I wonder—"

"I'll follow your money," said Tucker, which made no sense.

I laughed anyway and shoved my laptop on the bedside table, making room for my lap to get topped, completely unaware that in the morning, we'd learn of a dozen more deaths.

12

"Hope. Hope. Wake up!"

I cracked my eyes open. Sunlight. Argh.

I slammed my eyelids back shut, rolling onto my left side, away from Tucker, his tablet, and that infernal window. I rubbed my cheek into the cotton pillowcase, adjusting my course to avoid a small puddle of drool.

"Hope, we've got to get to the hospital, and I need you to see this!"

My eyes snapped open, heart bounding, as I surveyed the screen in front of my face.

EGYPT KILLS 12 SUSPECTS TWO DAYS AFTER TOURIST BUS BOMBED

"Sorry. I didn't mean to scare you, but this is nuts."

"I know." I grabbed Tucker's tablet and tried to assimilate the article.

Egypt's security forces had killed twelve "suspected fighters," in retaliation for the improvised explosive device that fatally wounded Phillip Becker and seriously injured Frederik Momberg and five other tourists.

Tucker crouched beside the bed and touched my hair. "There'll be a statement on state TV today, but we'll be working. I wanted you to know."

I shook off the last of the sleep fog. "Okay. All these men belonged to a group called Hasm, right? Looks like Hasm's affiliated with the Muslim Brotherhood."

"Yeah, but you see this part? 'Hasm and the Muslim Brotherhood both deny responsibility for this IED and condemn the government's actions.' It's weird, Hope. Hasm has claimed responsibility for other attacks, but not this one."

I twisted out of bed to brush my teeth and puzzle this out. "Could you turn on the TV while we're thinking? It's possible the BBC might have picked this up. We'll need maximum information to figure out who planted the IED."

Tucker flicked the switch, but kept his eyes on me instead of the screen as I brushed, spit, and flossed.

"What?" I demanded when I was done.

"Babe, I love you, and you're more amazing than any other woman on earth. But there's no way you're going to solve an IED blast in a foreign country. Do you even know what the Muslim Brotherhood is? Really?"

I rinsed my toothbrush with potable water from my stainless steel bottle. "Sort of. Can you boil it down to the YouTube version?"

Tucker broke into a grin. He relishes knowing more than me. "You remember Arab Spring in 2011?"

"Yes. Of course." I even retweeted some messages to amplify their voices, although I hadn't fully understood what was happening.

"It completely rocked the Middle East and forced out Egypt's president. Hosni Mubarak had been the president for almost thirty years. You know how crazy that was?"

"I have an idea." I grabbed a T-shirt and a pair of scrubs. I needed more long-sleeved shirts because of the rain.

"So Mohamed Morsi was elected in 2012 as only the fifth Egyptian president. He was an engineer and professor in California."

I smiled. My father's an engineer. So is Ryan Wu, which made Tucker promptly move on.

"Morsi was affiliated with the Muslim Brotherhood. He changed the constitution to give himself unlimited powers. He said that was to prevent Mubarek's judges from dissolving his constituency."

"Hmm. Was that true?"

"Hard to figure it all out from Canada. My friends weighed in on both sides. Anyway, Morsi did rescind those powers after people protested. Some journalists reported being targeted. But people kept protesting, and the military, the political opposition, and religious leaders all banded together for a coup. Morsi died in prison while under trial."

My mouth fell open. "How did he die?"

"Not a hundred percent sure. They said it was his diabetes, or maybe a heart attack. He was being held in Scorpion prison, which is supposed to be pretty inhumane."

"Whoa. That sounds ... wrong. The whole thing. I've never seen anyone die from diabetes."

"I have," said Tucker. "There was a 28-year-old alcoholic with diabetes who came in with diabetic ketoacidosis every week when I was working downtown. He died in DKA."

"I know children used to die of diabetes before Banting and Best discovered insulin, but that that was in the 1920s. I doubt the former president of Egypt was an alcoholic."

He waved to concede the point.

"And did you call it *Scorpion* Prison?"

He nodded. "The rest of the prison has a more normal name. I'd have to look it up. The entire complex is a political prison."

I sighed. "That's horrible. Who's the Egyptian leader now?"

"President el-Sisi."

I recognized the name after he said it. One of the med students had told me the Egyptian government "is good now, very stable." He'd neglected to explain its scorpion underbelly, which I should have researched myself.

A familiar female voice called from the TV. I turned to catch another clip of Karima Mansour at the IED site and immediately clicked the TV off.

When we climbed on the bus to the hospital, I clung to one of the overhead rails. Just like in Canada, people tended to clog up the front and refuse to move to the back. I whispered to Tucker, "I still don't feel like I understand the politics. At all."

"Join the club."

"I mean, I don't know who are the good guys or the bad guys, or if everyone's grey. I don't have a clue who bombed us and why." I glanced at him out of the corner of my eye. "We don't even know why we're here. Isabelle never told us."

Tucker grinned. "Well, I'm here to help people. For the rest of it, I'll ask around at work."

Easier said than done. I started off on the ambulatory side of the ER, tending to a five-year-old kid with a supracondylar fracture. She'd fallen while trying to climb a book case and brought it down on herself. She was lucky to have only one mildly-displaced fracture that should heal well.

"*In'sha'Allah*," said her mother.

I beamed and repeated, "*In'sha'Allah.*" It means "God willing," and is the first Arabic word I learned from patients in Montreal. It's like saying "with any luck," or "I hope so."

The little girl put up with a cast better than most Canadian five-year-olds. Then Rudy helped me enter some orders on Selsis, the electronic medical record system.

"Thanks, Rudy. It looks like SARKET, the EMR at St. Joe's, but better." When he grinned, I felt comfortable saying, "I have a non-medical question, if that's okay."

"Sure, sure. My pleasure."

I cleared my throat. "You remember the IED that, ah, affected Tucker and me on our first day?"

"Of course. We're so sad that it happened and grateful that you and Tucker were not harmed."

"Well, this morning we saw that the government had executed 12 people in retaliation. It seems awfully fast. I mean, it hasn't even been 48 hours since the IED—"

Rudy looked as if he'd swallowed a ghost pepper but was too polite to spit it out. "Ah, this is not medicine. This is politics."

"I know. I don't understand Egyptian politics, so that's why I'm asking you."

His eyebrows relaxed. "I see. Do you know what I think? It would be the best policy to leave it like that."

My turn to frown. "To leave it like what?"

"You're a tourist. You'll be back in Canada soon. Enjoy your freedom."

You mean ignorance? I thought, but he gave a little wave, signed up for the next chart, and disappeared into room 2.

Maybe Tucker would have better luck with him. It might be a guy thing.

Since approximately 40 patients waited to be seen, I didn't have the time or the nerve to try quizzing anyone else until lunchtime, when I lined up at the cafeteria for what smelled like fish and boiled peas.

Samira, the medical student, stood ahead of me in line. "How is your first day going?"

"Oh, it's interesting." I grabbed my plastic tray and a fork and took a deep breath of steamy air. "I have one awkward question, and I apologize if I'm not asking right. Did you hear about the government killing members of Hasm in retaliation for the tourist bus IED two days ago?"

"The terrorists?" she said, setting a napkin beside a knife and fork on her own tray.

"Um, are they terrorists?"

"They're all terrorists."

"Do you know Hasm?"

She swivelled her entire body to face me as her dark eyes bored into mine. "Excuse me. Do you think *I'm* a terrorist?"

"Of course not."

Even though a woman in a white uniform asked us what we wanted from behind the steel counter, Samira refused to answer. She kept watching me.

"I'm so sorry if I said it wrong. It's my first day. I definitely don't think you're a terrorist or anything like that. Please."

Samira kept staring at me until I was the one who looked away.

ny luck talking about the IED? I texted Tucker as I headed back to the ER, sans lunch. That exchange with Samira had ripped away my appetite.

Some.

With Rudy? I couldn't help asking

No, with some other guys. You?

Ha. I sent him a gif of Eddie Murphy locking his lips and waving 'bye.

My next patient was a woman with heavy and continuous periods. In Canada, the nurses might take bets on her hemoglobin. The lowest I've ever encountered was 60, which made them scoff. One nurse had seen one as low as 32.

This woman looked pale and tired and said she could barely walk, but no one joked about hemoglobin. I placed my orders (successfully!), and a lab tech came to draw the blood.

I saw a man with an ear infection that had ruptured his eardrum, a child with a large left lower pneumonia, and a guy with such a bad nosebleed that he'd bled through someone else's attempts at anterior packing. The staff doctor ended up installing two Foley catheters.

The last one made my hands shake. Blood everywhere. The

patient was a construction worker already known to have hepatitis C. There wasn't any protective gear on hand, not even gloves, and the staff doctor had pushed me aside to deal with it.

I belatedly realized that Canadians took their health for granted. Most people rushing to the ER's in London, Ontario or Montreal, Quebec have sore throats, colds, coughs, maybe a fracture. Most of them are quick to see and let go.

At this hospital, *everyone* was sick, even on the walk-in side. They didn't come unless they meant it.

"Go to lunch," said the staff, stripping off his gloves.

"I'm okay," I said. I felt a bit queasy anyway.

"Go to lunch," he repeated, and I went, texting Tucker to see if he was free. He was in acute care, seeing ambulance patients, so we might not cross paths at all.

I kept an eye out for the doctor with the broken nose, but I didn't spot any silver glasses. Maybe he wasn't scheduled to work, or maybe he'd needed some time off. I could understand either way.

In the still-steamy cafeteria, I grabbed an egg sandwich. Not my first choice, but I didn't want to line up again, and I couldn't survive the rest of my shift on a salad. I found an empty two-seater table by the window. The chocolate milk tasted a little different, but it quenched my thirst and boosted my energy.

Tucker slid into the black plastic seat across from me, beaming. "Hey, stranger."

"Good day?" I felt soul-crushed, but he looked exhilarated.

He leaned forward to brush a crumb off the corner of my mouth, and to whisper, "I helped deliver a baby! I mean, the social issues were tough because it was an unwed teen mother who'd denied her pregnancy, and she had FGM—"

"Female *genital* mutilation?"

"Right. I didn't realize how common it was in Egypt. Everyone else was surprised that I hadn't seen it before. I wasn't sure how to handle the delivery, so they helped me out."

I pressed my fist to my chest. That poor teenager. "I'm taking it was more than a clitoridectomy."

Tucker glanced from side to side to check if anyone was listening. "Tell you about it later."

"Right. Okay." We certainly weren't in Kansas anymore. "Grabbing lunch?"

He lowered his voice even more. "I'll get it after. Two things. I think I figured out what happened with Dr. Ahmed. The pathology resident."

The poor doctor with the broken nose. "You did? While you were delivering a *baby?*"

He waved his hand. "Not exactly. I was already texting people, asking questions."

Ah. The mysterious texts from last night when he tried to distract me by babbling about a quadfecta. At least he hadn't latched on a luscious belly dancer. Yet. "Okay. What was it?"

He beckoned for me to lean forward and practically pressed his lips against my ear. "Did you know how doctors are treated in Egypt?"

I shook my head.

"They went on strike in 2012. A police officer hit a physician who refused to falsify a medical report for him."

I jerked away from Tucker so fast that I almost rammed his nose. "Oh, my God. That's not—how could—"

In my mind's eye, I replayed the backs of two police officers casually walking away from cubicle number 5.

Tucker nodded at me. "You know what I'm saying. Police hit two other doctors in separate incidents. Plus physicians are working with unsterilized surgical equipment, without proper gloves. It's dangerous even if you're not assaulted."

I shuddered, remembering my nosebleed patient this morning.

"When they tell people to bring their own needles or cast material, the patients attack them too. Someone hit a female doctor and broke her jaw." Tucker gritted his teeth. "They're saying Dr. Ahmed was lucky that it was only a broken nose." He flashed me his phone. "You see this hospital bed?"

"What is that?" I recoiled from the photo. If I were a patient, I wouldn't even want to step on the dirty floor while wearing hip waders and a HAZMAT suit, let alone lie on that filthy mattress split down the middle, while paint and plaster flaked into my mouth.

Tucker wasn't done. "And it's only getting worse. Do you know how much each country's supposed to spend on health care?"

This, I knew from election debates in Canada. "We spend about 10 percent of our Gross National Product on health care, which is why they keep trying to cut it, but that's not possible with an aging population, more tests and treatment, and more technology."

Tucker sighed. "Last I saw was 11.7 percent in Canada. The U.S. is 17.7 percent. You know how much Egypt spends? They claim 3 to 5 percent, but my friends say that includes water and roads. So, like, when the nurses went on strike, they forced doctors to do the nursing jobs, and brought in nursing students. It's a hellhole."

Good God. I crumbled up my sandwich wrap, remembering all the Egyptian doctors and pharmacists who'd taught Tucker Arabic at McGill. "That must be why everyone wants to leave."

He nodded. "Half have left already, which makes it even worse for the ones who stay. It's dangerous here. Every day is like a war."

"I had no idea." I sat for a minute, stunned.

"I know. It's a lot. Sorry. I've got to get back and help, but first, I need to show you this." He flashed a pencil drawing at me. It took me a second to register what he'd done.

He'd drawn a portrait of the man who'd come out of the bathroom with Gizelda Becker.

It took my breath away. Tucker was good. Gifted, even. He'd once drawn a picture of me, and it was one of the things that had won my heart, even though we didn't discuss it.

"Amazing. Looks just like him."

Tucker grinned. "I snapped a picture of it and posted it on social media. My buddies will get the word out online."

"And you think they'll be able to find him in a city of 10 or 20 million people?"

Tucker shrugged. "Well. I am that good."

I grimaced before I laughed.

"He's also five foot eight, 150 pounds, and smells like Boss cologne."

"You have a better nose than me. Well, it's worth a try. Didn't people stalk a celebrity through Twitter?"

Tucker nodded. "Yeah. One of my friends told me there's an app we can use too."

"Freaky." There are apps for everything. "Okay, well, I've read *The Circle*. I hope things don't get too creepy."

He raised his eyebrows. Evidently our friend Tori hadn't persuaded him to read that book. "When have I ever been creepy?"

Part of being a good girlfriend is knowing when to smile reassuringly. "Rarely."

He caught my tone, but shrugged it off. "I gotta get something to eat before I fall over. You here for another ten?"

I checked my watch. "I'd better go. Love you."

He arched his eyebrows. "Not as much as *I* love *you*."

I heard a woman giggle behind us. It turned out to be a short, round-faced cleaner. I smiled back at her before I made a phone call to chase my own leads. I love Tucker, but a woman's got to solve her own cases.

14

One lead panned out immediately. That afternoon, Noeline Momberg and her kids stopped by our hospital with free coffee and pastries for everyone. I generally don't drink coffee, but I washed my hands in the cramped medication room and scooped up what looked like a shiny donut hole.

"They're called *zalabyas,*" Noeline told me, slapping Jaco's hands away from them. "We have to celebrate the fact that Papa's eyes are getting better."

"'Almost there,' right Mama? That's what Papa said." Fleur clapped her hands.

"Did the surgery go well, then?" I asked Noeline. I'd read that with penetrating injuries, like the metal in Frederik's right eye, only one fifth of patients ended up with better than 20/200 vision. Huge problem for a truck driver.

Noeline compressed her lips before she said, too loudly, "Coming along nicely. Every day is better. Please, have another *zalabya.*"

I slipped one to Jaco, who split it with Fleur.

Samira entered the med room, surveyed the treats now displayed on the counter between the sink and ice dispenser, and poured herself a coffee. "They're also called *loukmet el-qadi.*"

"I'll never remember that," I admitted, trying to act normal around her.

"It means 'the judge's food,'" said Samira, biting into one and smiling. "Thank you, madam. Medicine is a thankless job. And many of us are hungry."

Thankless? Hungry? In addition to getting beaten up and having your nose or jaw broken? The day just kept getting better.

I followed the Momberg family out of the med room while more doctors and nurses flocked toward the food. "Noeline, if there's anything we can do, please let us know. Don't feel like you need to bring us anything—"

"It's all from Ms. Becker. She asked us to bring it. She was supposed to meet us here." Noeline squirted hand sanitizer on Fleur and Jaco's hands.

"Ms. Becker?" I repeated. So they had become friends after all.

"I do apologize for my tardiness," called Gizelda Becker, crossing toward us from the nursing station. "How abominable of me to let you carry everything when you have two little children."

"You have so many things on your plate," said Noeline, although her lips seemed to turn down at the corners in agreement. "I have to get back to my husband now, but Jaco wanted to say hello to Dr. Tucker first."

The children waved and chewed, and even the exhausted staff smiled at their little faces. This wasn't a pediatric hospital, so cuteness made a welcome change.

Ms. Becker said, "I should let you get back to your work, and I do want to see Dr. Tucker."

"Absolutely. You'll find him on the acute side. How are you doing?" I didn't want to intrude on her grief.

She shook her head, her eyes unfocused. "I haven't had time to dwell on it. My brother keeps me hopping now that he's the only elephant."

I blinked at her.

"I'm sorry, I've been running everywhere since Wednesday. I'm not making sense." She passed a hand over her eyes. "We have a saying.

'When two elephants meet on a narrow bridge, they get nowhere until one of them backs down or lies down.'"

"I see." I did, actually. The bridge wouldn't magically expand for two pachyderms. One elephant had to go. Now that Phillip Becker had shuffled off this mortal coil, Luke would take over the bridge and boss his sister around.

"Before you go." My face flared red, but I pressed onward. "I heard that you and your father spoke often, and sometimes you would take notes."

"Where did you hear that?" She eyed me in a way that reminded me of a bald eagle: attentive, almost piercing.

I met her gaze, trying not to resemble a delicious herring or whatever eagles eat. "The other people on your tour group noticed your little red book."

She nodded slowly. "The Mombergs, of course. I see."

I willed the blush out of my cheeks. "Would you be willing to share your notes with us?"

"There's nothing in them. My father loved to talk, and he was accustomed to an audience, whether it was his secretary, some coworkers, or his family."

"Even so, Ms. Becker—"

"Gizelda, please."

My cheeks heated up even more. "Gizelda, sharing the notes could be a way of keeping your father's memory alive. I feel like I barely got to know him before he died. Sir William Osler said something like, 'Ask not what illness has the person, ask what person has the illness.'"

"Did he, now? Who is Sir William Osler?"

"He was a famous Canadian physician." I left out the dark side of Osler, namely "pimping." In medicine, that means questioning a learner to the point of ridicule. An observer wrote in 1916: *Rounded with Osler today. Riddles house officers with questions. Like a Gatling gun. Welch says students call it 'pimping.' Delightful.*

After a long moment, she shook her head. "The notes won't help you, Dr. Sze."

"Hope." I offered her my most charming smile.

Gizelda Becker gazed at me and pressed her lips together into a thin, bloodless line.

Hope is the thing with feathers
That perches in the soul ...

Gizelda shook her head before her phone binged in her purse. She ignored it. "You're a very persistent girl. Woman. Person."

"Thank you." I tried to scrape the question mark out of my voice. This didn't sound promising, Emily Dickinson notwithstanding.

"I appreciate your help here. You tried to save my father's life, and I think you and Dr. Tucker mean well. I should tell you, however ... " She paused. Her phone dinged again. She touched her purse, distracted.

I glanced at her purse myself. Who was trying to reach her? Probably Luke, but maybe it was the man with the cobra bag. *C'mon, answer it. Let me see your lock screen.*

Her fingers lingered on the zipper.

The phone started to ring with a loud, old school peal that reminded me of my grandma's house.

"I don't mind reading your notes, even if you think there's nothing in it." I raised my voice to be heard above the ring. "Sometimes it's comforting to share the words of your loved ones after they're gone."

She shook her head. "No, that's not it. You don't need to hear about Lord Carnarvon, or Osiris, or any of this."

"What about them?"

"Please, Dr. Sze. It's better for you, it's healthier—" She winced at her own phone's incessant bleating and walked away from me. She waved and called over her shoulder, "It's safer for you and Dr. Tucker to leave all of this alone. Please!"

15

"I could treat you to a cup of tea or coffee," said Muhamed, the tour guide from the bus, who wore a grey turban and caftan again today. He gestured toward a restaurant on the other side of the road, opposite the hospital. We'd have to cross a minimum of two smoggy lanes of traffic and two lanes of parked cars to get to it.

"Oh, I should treat you. I'm the one who invited you." I felt awkward without Tucker, who had to stay late to chart on the acute side, even though both of us had technically finished our shifts.

"You are my guest. Please." He stood still, waiting for me to decide. Despite the exhaust fumes and a siren in the distance, he emanated a sense of calm.

"That's okay. I don't really drink coffee or tea." I took a few deep breaths and migrated toward the shade of a lone tree. The rain had paused, and the sun briefly poked its head out.

Muhamed nodded gravely. "Would you like to go for a walk instead?"

I nodded. I'd have to carry my back pack, but I get depressed when I'm stuck in-hospital all day. "I'd also like to see the city, if that's okay. Dr. Tucker said he'll text me when he's done, maybe in the next half hour."

"Of course. I would be happy to see him."

As we walked along the sidewalk, trying to avoid the three inches of water that had accumulated in the road, I studied Muhamed's lean and weathered but sincere face. Just standing beside him felt good. He didn't feel pressured to chit chat. His calm somehow overrode the cacophony of a truck honking, a motorcycle beeping, and the construction grinding further up the block.

I took a deep breath—mistake. Smog—and began. "I've been trying to figure out what happened with the IED."

Muhamed inclined his head, thinking about it too. "Yes, I find it very troubling. We all pray the rest of the tourists will be well and that we may move on from this tragedy."

"Do you have clear memories leading up to the IED?"

"Yes, I was speaking into my microphone. I explained that the Grand Egyptian Museum contained an unprecedented number of artifacts, including the complete collection of King Tutankhamun, and had been built only two kilometres away from the Giza Pyramids. And then, the explosion."

"Where were you sitting?"

"I was sitting behind the driver, on the left."

The bus had caved in on the middle of the right side. Muhamed had been somewhat protected. Before I could pursue that thought, he added, "If only Allah had seen fit to hit my side instead of Mr. Becker's."

"Gosh, Mr. Muhamed, I don't think—"

"When a tourist dies, it is bad, very bad. But if an old Nubian man dies ... " He shrugged.

"You're not old." I'd guess he was 50, give or take a decade. "Your family would miss you very much."

He nodded. "That is true." He added a phrase in Arabic, and I thought I caught the word Allah. "It was His will that you and Dr. Tucker were there."

"Oh. I'm glad you think so. I was trying my best to look after Mr. Becker. His daughter said he was talking about—" I hesitated, then decided to go for it. "A mongoose and treasure. Do you know what a mongoose is?" I held up my phone, ready with a picture of what, to me, looked like a brown ferret or a weasel with tiny, sharp teeth, standing on its hind legs.

His eyebrows lifted toward his turban. "Rudyard Kipling wrote about Rikki-tikki-tavi, a grey mongoose who becomes the pet of a British family in India. He said they're very curious."

"Right! I remember Rikki-tikki-tavi killing the cobras that threatened their baby. Do you know of mongoose—mongooses—in Egypt?"

He tilted his head to the side. "It's possible. I've not heard of them in Cairo."

"You do have cobras, though?"

"There is an Egyptian cobra, sometimes called an asp, which was most famously implicated in Cleopatra's death, although scholars say this may be more legend than fact. The Egyptian cobra is the second largest cobra on the continent of Africa." He chuckled at my face. "Don't worry, Dr. Sze. I have never seen a cobra except at the Giza Zoo. Even the scorpions don't like Cairo. Too busy!"

I forced a laugh. I've been checking my running shoes every morning regardless.

"As for treasure, you have to remember that ancient Egypt lies beneath our feet. Modern Egypt was built on top of it. We've located 30 percent of Egyptian monuments, but 70 percent are still underground. We're still finding monuments in Aswan or Heliopolis," he said.

Oh, he was good. He'd anticipated exactly where I was going.

"Many tourists assume we've already found everything, particularly in Cairo, but did you hear about the 26-foot statue of King Psamtik I, extracted from the mud in 2017?"

I shook my head.

"It made international headlines. *Colossal quartzite statue of ancient Egypt's most powerful ruler pulled out of the mud of a Cairo slum!* They believed it was a depiction of Pharaoh Ramses II, but later learned it honored King Psamtik I, who came to power in 664 BC, uniting the empire by seizing control of Upper Egypt from the Nubian Twenty-

Fifth Dynasty, fighting off Libyan marauders, and encouraging Greek settlers."

My brain balked, trying to harness all these facts, and paused on one I could grasp. "How could you hide 26 feet of statue in a Cairo slum?"

"The reporters called it a slum or a working class neighborhood, Dr. Sze. I would call it El Matareya." The syllables rolled off his tongue. "You'll find it east of the Nile, in the northern part of Greater Cairo, closer to the airport. During the Pharaohs' reign, Matareya formed part of the ancient city known as On in the Hebrew Scriptures, later called Heliopolis by the Greeks. It's the site to worship the sun gods known as Atum and Ra, sometimes merged and called Ra-Atum or Atum-Ra."

"Wow." I paused to absorb the most Egyptian history of my life and was startled to see at least six grey, skinny cats with white bellies and legs who were leaning in the shade of a short concrete wall. I admired them but didn't dare approach them as I tried to formulate my thoughts. "So I guess there are a lot of archaeologists in Matareya."

Muhamed smiled and shook his head. "Far more ordinary people live in the area. In southern Cairo, the archaeological site of al-Ma'adi, which predated even the pharaohs—has been turned into a car park."

I gasped. One cat zipped further down the wall, as if I'd scared it. Two others stared at me.

"Yes, and looting is everywhere. An entire tomb was taken from the Giza Plateau in 2014. So to answer your question briefly, Dr. Sze, we have many treasures in Egypt, but even more people who want to relieve us of them."

Guilt stabbed me. Tucker and I wanted treasure too, but the antiquities here already belonged to the people. The heat seemed to rise off the wet pavement and steam my skin. "I understand."

He tilted his head from side to side. "It's funny, I didn't hear Mr. Becker talking about a mongoose. Or treasure."

"Oh! You understand Afrikaans?"

He nodded as one cat yawned and began licking its paws. "To some extent. I was a translator before I became a tour guide. My focus is mainly on Arabic and English, but I developed a basic understanding of a few other languages in order to facilitate relationships."

"Wonderful." Embarrassment flooded through me. I had never asked this distinguished man why he spoke such good English. Of course it would be adaptive for an Egyptian to learn maximal languages in a tourist-based economy.

"He was mainly talking about his bad luck," said Muhamed, ignoring my discomfort.

A cat, slightly bigger than the others, stared past me and hissed, revealing its sharp canines.

"His bad luck," I repeated blankly.

The fierce cat's tail twitched. A car honked, as if in reply.

"'We are so unlucky.' 'This is all my fault.' 'I knew this would happen.' 'I never should have done it.'"

I perked up. "Never should have done what?"

He shook his head and checked the time. "I didn't hear an explanation." He smiled at the cats. "Did you know the first kitten was named Nedjem, which means 'sweetness' or 'sweet one'? It lived during the reign of Thutmose III, which ended in 1425 BCE." Then he beckoned me to turn back toward the hospital, leaving the cats behind.

"Cute. I mean, how sweet." I struggled to make a nice segue back to the IED and gave up on subtlety. "Did you hear Mr. Becker say the word Kruger?"

Muhamed shook his head and ushered me to the inward part of the sidewalk as an overburdened truck drove by with a mattress tied to its roof. The truck's wheels splashed his legs. "No, but I had others to care for. We wanted to bring the ambulances and the police in without too much coverage from the media. He did say something about his hand."

Hmm. I hadn't noticed anything wrong with Mr. Becker's hand, but I might've been distracted by the nail in his head.

I sighed. The most obvious explanation why Mr. Becker was "so unlucky" and "never should have done it"? The bombed bus. Dead end. Literally.

I shielded my face from raindrops that had started to fall once again. "Thanks for your help, Muhamed."

"You're welcome, Dr. Sze. It's an honour to help you."

I half-laughed. "An honour?" Maybe his English wasn't quite as good as I'd imagined.

He smiled at me as the hospital's palm trees came back into our view. "I should also mention that my granddaughter likes to follow you on Instagram."

"Oh!"

"She says your brother maintains the page, but even so. We enjoy your adventures."

That made my cheeks burn. "You knew who I was before we met?"

"No, not me. I didn't know your name until I met you on the bus, but she was excited to see you on the news. She may even have followed your page before that."

"See, that's very strange to me. I don't know how old your granddaughter is, but why would she be interested in a Canadian doctor?"

He chuckled. "A Canadian crime-fighting doctor. She says you're better than reality TV, and that you have some very funny TikToks."

Thanks, Kevin. "Ah. Thank you."

My phone buzzed with a text from Tucker: *Almost done. Meet you in 10.*

Muhamed raised his voice above the traffic. "Dr. Sze, I remember one other thing Mr. Becker said. It was something about a body."

"A body?" I squeaked. Then I caught myself. "You mean his own body, because he was hurt?"

"Ah, no. Perhaps my language skills are not ... if I understand correctly, he was referring to the body of a god."

"A god's body. As in a corpse?"

Muhamed gestured one graceful brown hand in the air. "I'm not certain. I apologize if I'm confusing the issue. He was muttering, and the sirens were so loud. I may have misinterpreted it all. Please forgive me."

"Not at all. Thank you so much for taking the time to see me."

He grinned. "The pleasure is all mine. Would it be too much trouble to ask you for a selfie of us together? My granddaughter was asking."

"Sure, if you want." I have no idea why strangers want pictures of me, but I'm cool with it. "I have one last question, though. Did Mr. Becker mention money?"

He frowned. "Money?"

"Yes. A ... collection of money." I'd already mentioned Kruger. I didn't want to say "millions," but I couldn't resist pointing him in the right direction.

"No, nothing about that."

And then we took six different selfies. Somehow, although he insisted his granddaughter would be delighted, I looked strained in all of them.

16

No sign of Tucker as we approached the hospital.

Muhamed wouldn't leave me alone on the sidewalk. "It's best not to leave a young woman unaccompanied."

I checked my watch, trying not to notice that I was thirsty, tired, and now getting rained on, while car engines roared in my ears. "It's not even 6 p.m."

"It happens in broad daylight." Muhamed hesitated. "I'm afraid that foreign women can be at higher risk."

"Higher risk?"

He looked pained. "There have been complaints of harassment against women. We don't see this on my tours, of course. We keep you very safe."

Now my fatigue mingled with a bit of fear. I'd never been alone in Egypt. My post-bomb adrenaline had ebbed, and my knees sagged. Time to sleep. Stat.

Muhamed walked me into the lobby. Then he bowed slightly and said something in Arabic, which he explained meant goodbye, but also "go in peace 'very much.'"

Although the hospital air smelled slightly like stale sweat and body spray, the doors sealing behind me also minimized the noise and pollution. Mixed blessing.

I yawned and texted Tucker. *You ready? I'm done.*

Almost, he wrote back.

So I wouldn't fall asleep in front of the security guards, I perched on a wooden bench beside my back pack and made notes on my phone.

Becker: mining. Treasure. Mongoose. Lord Carnarvon. Osiris. My fault. I shouldn't have done it. Kruger millions?

Why did Gizelda Becker give away PB's cobra pouch?

Why did Sarquet Industries pay for our trip?

A body. The body of a god.

All of this could be important, or none of it.

I tried not to resent Tucker. Medicine is a harsh mistress. And Ryan never complained when he waited for me.

Googling "god body" pointed me to a conspiracy theory, so I added the key word "Egypt." This led to Egyptian mythology. I clicked on Osiris. His name kept coming up. Why?

"Hope!" Tucker hustled to my side twenty minutes later, laughing at my screen. "You checking out green dudes now? I better buy some body paint."

I touched his arm, but avoided kissing him, so as not to offend any pious onlookers. The springy curls of hair on his arm cheered me up a tad. "Hey. Are you telling me you don't recognize this guy, so I know more about Egyptian history than you? Score."

He raised his eyebrows at me. "Never! I present to you Osiris, Egypt's Lord of the Underworld. Judge of the Dead. His name means 'powerful.'"

"Okay, I'll give you two points for that and take away one for tardiness."

"Sorry. Charting, then Dr. Sharif—"

"Dr. Mostafa Sharif? You finally got to meet the chief of the ER? What's he like?"

Tucker shrugged. "He seemed like a nice guy. He wanted to meet you, actually."

I flinched and dropped my phone in my pocket. Laziness is a cardinal sin in medicine. "You tell him my shift was over?"

"Yeah, I said you'd already stayed late, but had an appointment, and you'd be in first thing tomorrow." He frowned. "I was a little surprised he showed up. Friday's the holy day in Islam."

I groaned. Tucker and I had been scheduled for the same shift hours, but acute care means more complicated cases, so he'd stayed late to chart, which meant he'd met the chief of ER. Everything conspired to make me look like a giant sloth bag.

"Don't stress. You'll knock 'em dead tomorrow. What'd you find about my man O?"

It took me a second to realize Tucker was making a joke about Osiris, not orgasms, although the way his brown eyes twinkled, it was yet another double entendre.

I drew him away from a man pushing a cleaning cart. "I guess it all started with the sun god, or gods, who created the world. Side bar: Muhamed told me that there used to be a huge Atum-Ra worship site northeast of Cairo."

"Yeah. Heliopolis, right? They found a giant statue, but they're fighting a losing battle against looters." Tucker smiled and nodded at the cleaner, who nodded back.

"How did you know that?"

"I know everything." Tucker dabbed, an iconic dance move which is so over that Kevin groans if he catches it on YouTube.

The cleaner dabbed back, left arm bent, right arm toward the sky.

Okay, maybe it's not over in Egypt. We both grinned and waved at the cleaner while I said, "I don't know why Osiris gets top billing in this story, because a lot of the plot comes down to his wife."

Tucker winked at me. "Yep, behind every great man lies an Isis. And I don't mean the terrorist group."

"Shh!" Pretty sure ISIS wasn't a joke here. "I mean the five thousand-year-old *goddess* Isis."

"Who saved her brother-husband's life."

I grimaced. "Yeah, they really did marry their siblings. Kept the wealth and power concentrated in the royal family."

Tucker held out his arms. I nestled against him as he patted my head and said, "Don't worry. We're not related."

"Praise be." A mother in a head scarf glanced at us and pulled her three children closer to her, so I disengaged from Tucker and towed him toward the door, even though I knew I'd have to yell over the traffic.

Sure enough, the doors opened to a wave of humidity, rain, and noise, as I asked, "Did you know that Osiris and Isis had three siblings?"

Tucker shook his head. "Two, right?"

"No, actually. The five kids were Osiris, Isis, Set, Nephthys, and Horus the elder. Anyway, King Osiris and Queen Isis led Egyptian civilization to new levels of art and agriculture. And then wham!"

Tucker's forehead pleated, partly in response to the jackhammering in a nearby apartment. "Remind me."

"Well, there are different versions. To them, written words had the power of creation, so they didn't write down the really terrible stuff."

Tucker sniffed the air. We'd turned left instead of right, and food carts dotted the main road.

Barbecued meat smelled mighty tempting, even as a neo-vegetarian. I distracted myself with the story. "In one version, Nephthys dressed up like Isis and seduced Osiris. He thought he was sleeping with his wife, but he was—"

Tucker raised his eyebrows. "Banging his *other* sister?"

"Who was also his sister-in-law. Nephthys had married Set. Now, Set had always been jealous, but when he ran into his brother-king and Nephthys's flower fell out of Osiris's hair—"

"Boom," Tucker said.

"Right. Revenge time. Set threw a party and displayed a magnificent, custom-made wooden chest. Everyone took turns lying inside it. The chest fit Osiris perfectly. Then Set locked King Osiris in it and threw it in the Nile."

"Hold up. You can't just lock the king in a box and toss him in the closest river."

"Apparently, you can. King Osiris drowned in that coffin chest."

"Whoa." Tucker ran a hand through his bangs, which had started to flop despite his usual gel.

A cheerful woman bicycled past us, pushing what appeared to be a small library attached to the front of her bike.

Tucker lowered his voice so the cyclist couldn't hear. "People keep talking about Osiris."

"Yes. Phillip Becker kept bringing him up."

Tucker bent to whisper in my ear. "And now you're telling me that Osiris was a victim of murder."

17

I shivered. Part of it was Tucker's proximity, his breath and his voice in my ear.

And part of it was his question. Was it possible that Mr. Becker had been deliberately killed, like Osiris?

IEDs are planted to kill, maim, and incite fear. But what if this had been a targeted attack?

Three kids in a passing car goggled at us.

Leave me alone. I cleared my throat and stepped away from Tucker. I'm not comfortable trapped in an urban zoo.

I flew out of Canada to escape the "detective doctor" label, but in Cairo, a grandpa recognized me from Instagram, and everyone treated us like free TV when we walked down the street.

I'd ask Kevin to scale back on social media. He thinks we should exploit my fame. *They're selling newspapers and toothpaste ads off your story. Why shouldn't you get some?*

I'd agreed, partly because our parents had invested so much in my education that I wanted to pay it back, even through minimal ad revenue. Right now, with student debt threatening to sink my battleship, all I had to offer was "cool story, bro." But infamy made me anxious and irritable, especially so far from home.

If I didn't sleep soon, I'd explode.

"You okay, Hope?" Tucker's brow creased.

I shrugged. You never show weakness in medicine. "Long day. Let's go back to the hotel. We should research Mr. Becker more. Figure out if someone wanted him dead, especially if he had 'treasure.'"

"Agreed. Let's grab some eats, and you keep telling me the Osiris and Isis story."

"You think street food is okay?" I raised my eyebrows at the first food "cart," a small wooden table on the sidewalk. The table supported a portable stove where two pots bubbled with unappetizing contents.

The cart man nodded at me, a short woman beckoned us, and a taller woman pointed to the purple Arabic sign tacked to the side of their silver car.

"Hello, yes, very safe. Come eat!" called the man.

I shook my head. *Let's go.*

"Cool. What do you have?" said Tucker, ignoring me tugging on his arm.

"Delicious lentils with tomatoes and toasted bread! We also have *belila,* Egyptian wheat berries. Or you could try hummus, tea, or *qaraa assaly,* which is Egyptian pumpkin pie."

Well. That sounded pretty good, with one exception. "No wheat berries," I muttered. My parents used to force oatmeal and cream of wheat on me, inducing a lifelong horror of gloopy grains.

"We're very careful about hygiene," said the shorter woman, smiling. "I work in the insurance industry, my husband is an engineer, and our friend works at a bank."

"And you run a food truck too?" said Tucker.

"It's necessary to send our children to school," said the bank friend, whose head scarf matched her fancy pink nails.

I'd hidden my money in the thigh pouch with the ankh, which made it awkward to access cash on the street, but Tucker insisted on buying it all, even the wheat berries.

"Could you please try them now? If you don't like them, we can adjust the recipe," said the man.

"If you do like them, we are on Instagram, Twitter, Facebook, and Snapchat," said the cheery insurance woman. "Could we take a picture of you?"

I winced and said, "It's been a long day," but Tucker chirped, "Sure!"

I kept my head down while I sampled everything. Even the wheat berries. Verdict: less horrendous than my parents' oatmeal. Wheat berries literally tasted like wheat, maybe with a hint of pine nuts. I liked the toppings of pomegranate seeds and what turned out to be dried cherries in a coconut-milk sauce.

"You are students!" said the insurance woman. "You should eat this every day. This is the hot cereal for all Egyptians, as well as our 'sohoor' during Ramadan, eating this before dawn to sustain us throughout our day of fasting."

Awesome. Maybe it would sustain me back to the hotel.

The lentils didn't taste like much, so I mixed in some hummus, which upped the yum factor. Plus, no one ever complains about pumpkin pie. This one was almost like a custard, which was great, except I can't stand raisins.

"Please leave us good reviews. Our children's future depends on it. We want to buy a proper food cart, and licensing is so expensive!" said the insurance mom.

When we finally tore ourselves away, their card in hand, loaded down with leftovers, a bearded, bespectacled, twenty-something man at a neighboring bicycle cart food stand called, "Please! I make the best koshary!"

"World famous homemade burgers! Hot dogs! Hawawshi!"

"Chinese food! Sweet and sour chicken. Rice. Linguini!"

"Nutella tangine! Cake pops! Brownies!"

"I want to go home. We have enough," I said. I love food, but I needed to drink water somewhere cool and quiet.

"Just a minute." Tucker hailed the koshary guy, who seemed to be named Ali. Ali's koshary looked like more lentils in a tomato sauce, although both Ali and Tucker swore that the fried onions made it special.

"We'll take it home and eat it for breakfast," said Tucker, raising his voice to tell the other food carts, "Don't worry. We'll be back! We'll be eating every day!"

If you don't get sick, I thought. No guarantees. My family prides itself on a cast iron stomach. My dad once advised me not to throw away old, stinky noodles, unless they still smelled rotten *after* I heated them up. It worked for me, but Tucker has a more vulnerable GI tract.

I zoned out until Tucker said, "Thirty percent unemployment for people our age. Can you imagine, Hope?"

I shook my head, eyelids drooping. My shoulders ached from my back pack. My arms felt weighed down by the food 'cause I'm a wimp. I unstuck my tongue from the roof of my mouth and swallowed the little saliva I had left.

Ali glanced at me with sympathetic brown eyes. "Are you okay?"

Tucker pocketed his change for the koshary. "Wow. I had no idea Nasser made university education so accessible, but then you had no jobs after."

I fantasized about Ryan Wu, who not only carried my back pack without being asked, but never socialized away my precious hours of free time. We did church stuff for God, not because Ryan loved hanging out over cookies and lemonade.

I could almost taste the cold bottle of drinkable water I'd left in the hotel fridge.

I am going to kill you, Tucker.

Tucker continued, oblivious, "Well, EMR's a growing field, right? We just got electronic records at our hospital in Montreal."

"SARKET," I snorted to myself. What a gong show. Working with that system on a graveyard shift marked one of the worst nights of my life. And for me, that's saying something.

Ali brightened. "Yes, SARKET. I worked on it myself as a student, in development, five years ago. Was it not a successful implementation?"

I gaped at him. Even Tucker shut up.

Finally, I said to Ali, "You helped develop SARKET, the electronic medical system at St. Joseph's Hospital in Montreal, Canada?"

Ali blinked. "I believe so. Our company planned an international expansion, including Canada. Was your software made by Sarquet Industries?"

18

arquet was spying on us.

    I couldn't breathe for a second as every instinct locked up on me.

Those mofos recorded every word I wrote at St. Joe's, and then they brought me over here.

No. I forced myself to exhale and switch to logic mode.

I don't write anything personal on EMR. It's patient information like *13 y.o. girl with asthma. Chief Complaint: Knee pain.* Plus it's all supposed to be encrypted so outsiders, including the software developers, can't access it.

Still. The fact that they could potentially have read our reports, and factored that into inviting us on a free trip, felt Big Brother to me.

I'd researched Sarquet Industries before accepting the trip. Or at least I'd checked the Wikipedia stub and media releases, since I couldn't dig up much on a private corporation based in the Middle East and Asia, although they claimed a 2.5 percent share of the worldwide market.

"Why did they hide their name? Sarquet Industries vs. Selsis and SARKET," I said out loud. Isabelle never volunteered that Sarquet owned the EMR both at St. Joe's and at the Cairo hospital they'd chosen for us. Multiple names and slightly different systems had thrown me off.

Ali adjusted a stack of plates on his cart, uncomfortable. He had beautiful, slender hands, with a gold ring on his ring finger. "I believe their names were inspired by Serket, the Egyptian goddess. It's spelled Serqet, Selket, Selqet, and Selcis."

Sure, spellings vary in translation from different scripts or characters. But companies usually stick to one brand name.

What was Sarquet Industries playing at?

Why did they want us here?

"And why Serket," I muttered under my breath. They referenced Egyptian mythology right after Tucker asked me about Osiris's murder. Coincidence? My head spun, and not only because I needed aqua.

As if reading my mind, Ali handed me a bottle of water.

"No, thanks." We'd already spent enough. Water would be cheaper at a corner store.

"It's a gift."

I set my bags of food on the ground and took the bottle, my fingertips erasing the condensation on the sides. I popped open the lid and felt better with one sip.

"Egypt is a desert. Please make sure you drink enough throughout the day. Now tell me, why did Sarquet Industries invite you here?"

I felt embarrassed explaining our free trip when they wouldn't give him a job, but the man had handed me water. I told him the truth.

"Strange," Ali said, without rancor.

"You're not angry?"

He raised his eyebrows. "Of course. But that serves no purpose. I would be more likely to land a job if I made friends with you and made a connection to Isabelle Antoun or Youssef through you, you see?"

That made me feel better. I downed half the bottle and felt my eyes clear and my shoulders relax.

Tucker kissed my temple and took my bags of food. "Sorry, babe. I should keep a better eye on you."

"I can keep an eye on myself." Although I'd nearly failed on that score. I turned to Ali. "We don't know why they invited us. That's the truth. I've asked them a zillion times. No straight answers. A lot of inviting us out on tours." My cheeks reddened. What they'd already spent on us could feed Ali's family for a month. "I'm sorry. I can ask them if they have any openings."

Tucker held up his phone. "I connected with him on LinkedIn, Hope, and I'll bring up his c.v. with Isabelle and Youssef."

I still felt beholden for the water. "Let me see what I can do for you too."

"We're on your team," said Tucker.

"And I'm on yours." Ali fist bumped him, slightly awkward with plastic bags of food looped over Tucker's wrists. Ali said, "Now take your woman home. She works hard and needs a rest."

I smiled at Ali. "I'm okay, but thank you."

We walked toward the bus stop while Tucker waved and called out to more food cart owners.

At the bus stop, we claimed a wet but empty green plastic bench. I felt more relaxed despite the omnipresent honks and the soot no doubt clogging my nose.

I offered Tucker a sip of water and checked my phone. "He's right."

Tucker glugged the rest of the water down and crumpled the bottle before kissing my cheek. "Thanks. I'm always right."

Shoot. I was still thirsty, not to mention annoyed at his attitude. *I am magnificent! I'm always right!* "No, I mean Ali. Selsis and SARKET are both made by Sarquet Industries. You think it's a coincidence that shortly after St. Joe's installed SARKET, our hospital can barely function, leaving Sarquet free to fly us out to Egypt?"

Tucker frowned. "Hang on. You can't blame your graveyard shift on Sarquet Industries. That was a completely different disaster."

"Yeah, but everyone hates SARKET. I mean, Tori never complains about anything, and she wrote a full page of problems that need fixing."

"True." He moved the bags to the right so he could squeeze closer to me. "I'm not hyping SARKET. It's going better, though. And I love St. Joe's, but they never implement anything right."

I nodded. The entire Quebec health system broils in incompetence. Canada divides health care up by province, and it never ceases to amaze me, the difference between my home province, Ontario, vs. its neighbor, Quebec. Although health care is precarious everywhere now, from what my friends tell me.

I breathed in the smog and longed for more water, but we should bus back to the hotel soon. "Still. It seems wrong that Isabelle never told us they'd installed our EMR when they invited us here. Why would you hide that?"

"Agreed."

"It feels like they're watching us." I shifted on the bench, which had already soaked my scrubs. I should've sat on one of the plastic bags, or my back pack.

"We can call them right now if you want," said Tucker.

My head began pounding at both temples. "Nah. I've got a headache."

"Okay. First thing tomorrow morning. Before our shift."

"Awesome." I don't sleep well before confrontation, but maybe jet lag would make up for it. I yawned.

"Plus Ali's going to help us out. He thinks he can help ID the guy with the cobra bag, too."

I straightened up, my knee knocking into Tucker's. "He recognized him?"

"Said he looked familiar. And I'm getting some nibbles on Twitter. I'm telling you, Hope, you can go to sleep. I've got this. Tuck-ah's in the houuuuuuse."

That snapped me awake. *You've* got this? What am I, steamed lentils? I reached for my phone.

"What are you doing?" said Tucker.

"I'm texting Muhamed."

"You got a lead, huh?" He nudged my elbow and grinned. "That's so cute."

"Cute?" I wanted to bash him with my phone. Only that would hurt my phone.

"What? It's a compliment. I love the way you're like a dog with a bone." He nuzzled my cheek.

I shoved his shoulder. *"You've* got this, *you're* in the houuuuuuuse, you drink all my water, and I'm the cute, little *dog?"*

"Huh?"

I enunciated every word to make this clear. "You're the magnificent Sherlock Holmes, and I'm your elementary doggy Watson who should go to *sleep?"*

He held up his hands. "Hey. Don't worry, Hope. We all know you're the 'detective doctor.'" He actually held up his fingers to do air quotes. "I know you're thirsty and tired and pissed off that you didn't get to meet the chief of ER. But I'm doing my best to feed you and get you home."

I inhaled. *I love this guy.*

Exhaled. *But I can't stand him right now.*

I looked him straight in the eye. "Don't pretend you're the hero."

"What?"

I pointed at the crunched water bottle in his lap. "I told you I wanted to go home. Multiple times. But you kept talking and talking."

"What? Really? I didn't hear you."

"Because you're too busy making friends with everyone. It's pathological. *You're* the one always wagging your tail. *I speak Arabic! I'm the best! Love me, love me, love me!* You take ten years to do anything because you've got to shake hands with all creatures great and small."

Tucker opened his mouth and then closed it. He knew I was right.

My voice cracked. "You're so into *them,* you don't care if I've been sprayed with toilet water, or jet lagged, or stressed out from the IED and an ER shift."

Tucker's eyes widened. "Oh. Right. I didn't think."

"You finished my water without asking me. The water Ali gave to *me* while you were talking and talking."

"Shit. Hope—"

"And then you condescend to me about being the 'detective doctor' and tell me to go to sleep?" I added the air quotes myself.

"I'm just—" He paused, and even in the rapidly-encroaching darkness, his cheeks flushed. "Well, of course I want to figure out what's going on. And I have to drink water."

"You can drink water, but every time we get a case, you try to run with it and leave me in the dust."

Tucker drew back, shaking his head. "Maybe that time with Elvis—"

"Every. Time."

He paused to think about it before he gave a slight nod. "Well, I can see how you might look at it that way."

"Every. Time. And you need to be loved by everyone. It never stops. Tonight the *street vendor* could tell I was thirsty and tired, but you kept going on and fucking on. Even after Ali pointed it out to you. Even after I told you I have a headache. So no, I don't think it's *cute* that you want to be the 'detective doctor.' Who the fuck are you, anyway?"

Tucker opened his mouth and shut it a few times. By the time the bus came, blinding us with its lights, he still hadn't said a word.

19

A silent Tucker was a strange beast.

In a way, it was refreshing. I still throbbed with the mean pleasure of telling him off as I slid in the window seat and turned toward the glass.

I felt the weight of him settling on the aisle seat beside me, but didn't turn to acknowledge him until I detected a different cologne, and my seat mate called, *"Konnichi wa!"*

I whipped my head around and spotted Tucker still standing in the aisle with the food bags wrapped around both wrists, eyes wide, before I rotated to stare at the man directly beside me.

He was young. Young enough not to have much of a mustache. But he seemed plenty confident and maybe drunk as he singsonged to me in pseudo Japanese and placed a hand on my left knee.

In that moment, it hit me that a) I'd taken a seat on the right side of the bus, the same side where Mr. Becker had been killed, and b) I was trapped by some douche.

I seized his hand, threw it in his lap, and stood up.

The guy stood up too, laughing as he blocked me. He cupped his hands in the air like he was squeezing a pair of breasts or my rear end.

"Try it and die," I said. "Now get out of my way."

The guy chortled and air-squeezed again. Honk honk.

Tucker growled something at him in Arabic, leaning toward him.

The guy threw up his hands and oozed between me and Tucker, heading further down the aisle. "Sorry, sorry," he said to Tucker in English.

Why should he apologize to Tucker? He hadn't grabbed Tucker's knee.

"Fuck yourself," I told the douche, but not too loud. I didn't want to get tossed into an Egyptian prison.

Tucker dropped into the seat next to me, piling the food in his lap. "You okay? He came out of nowhere."

I rolled my eyes. "My knee will survive. I wish I could smash his face, though."

"Me too," said Tucker. "We okay?"

I shrugged.

"Am I better than that guy?"

"Marginally." I allowed, and when he offered to take my hand, I wrapped my fingers around his.

"Maybe we should spring for a taxi or Uber-Careem next time. The two ride share companies merged," he explained, but that wasn't the crucial part to me.

"What? You're suggesting taking a car?"

"You're allowed, after an IED, an international flight, a toilet spray, and a full ER shift. Sorry, I'm worried about money."

I nodded but remembered the cash he'd spent on food tonight. And the roses.

"Every morning, I wake up and tell myself I'm not going to spend anything. But when I talk to Egyptian people about unemployment, I just ... " He shook his head and stared at the bags in his lap.

"I get it. And we have to eat. But I don't want to spend all night joking with your new friends on the street. I have to sleep, and I don't want you to shame me for it."

"Shame you?"

"Yeah. In medicine, you're shamed for eating or sleeping or going to the bathroom. It's crazy that we're supposed to take care of everyone else 24/7, but we're weak if we take a few seconds for ourselves."

Tucker nodded. After a minute, he said, "I've got to think about this."

"Okay." I squeezed his hand. "I'm sorry if I was hard on you. My head does hurt. And you did get rid of that douche bag."

"You're welcome," he said, before he reverted to silence again.

Fear welled in my chest—*he's mad at me, he's going to leave me, I already lost Ryan, Tucker and I are fundamentally incompatible*—but I breathed in and out and studied his face. He flashed me a quick smile that didn't touch his eyes.

No, we weren't okay yet. Still, I didn't have to deal with a strange guy sing-songing fake Japanese and grabbing my knee.

Part of me wanted to stay awake in case another IED hit.

The other part of me thought, *If a bomb hits, I'd better rest up first. And my body will shield Tucker's.*

Hope the douche gets it, though.

I nodded off against the window, despite the loud conversations swirling around me. At least they weren't playing music this time.

I jolted awake when the bus hit a bump.

"You okay?" Tucker grabbed the bags and me, in that order.

I blinked. "Are we there?"

"Not yet." He patted my hair. "You can sleep some more."

My mouth and eyes had both dried out, and pain still drummed a steady rhythm in my temples. "I guess I'm up now."

"You want food?"

I shook my head. "I'll eat when we get back."

"You want a story to put you to sleep?"

I smiled. "Kinky. Yes, but first you can tell me if that douche is still around, without making it obvious."

"He got off on the last stop."

"Thank goodness." I yawned and surveyed the bus, pleased by the lack of douche. "Okay. What's your story?"

"I was looking up Serket, the scorpion goddess."

"Why?"

He shrugged and, for no reason, my heart melted. I kissed his cheek.

He kissed mine, still subdued. "I love you."

"I love you too." My eyes told him I wished we could touch more in public, and his eyes gleamed back before he changed the subject.

"I read about Sarquet Industries, and I decided to research the goddess for clues. Did you know she's the goddess of medicine?"

"Oh, that's cool. It also makes more sense why they'd name a medical record system after her."

"And their whole corporation, yeah. Her name literally means 'she who causes the throat to breathe.'"

"Kind of an odd way to phrase it when scorpions can kill you, right?"

He shrugged. "Not usually adults. I looked that up too. There are 1500 scorpion species, but only about 25 are dangerous to us. Breathing problems, arrhythmias, paralysis and death. Kids might die, and anyone who's allergic. Usually it's more painful than anything else."

"Huh. Well, it still seems backward to name the scorpion goddess as the goddess of medicine, but I'm a fan of breathing." I no longer take my respiratory system for granted after people have tried to strangle me.

"They used to paint her with the scorpion on her head, its tail standing erect and ready to sting. They didn't want their goddess to be powerless."

"I'm a fan of power." And I knew what standing erect meant to him.

"I know you are." He winked at me. "She's a good goddess for you."

Well, I could handle being compared to a goddess. Even if—especially if—she did sting. I laughed. "Did you know my astrological sign? I'm a Scorpio." I turned 27 on November seventh.

"See? It's fate. I don't know if Serket ties into Osiris and Isis, though. I didn't have a chance to read about them."

I blinked, still adjusting to the light. "Oh, I can tell you that." I deepened my voice like a movie announcer. "When Set took over the throne with Nephthys as his consort, the desert winds blew. The land turned barren. Brother turned against brother, and the world collapsed into war."

"Brother had already turned against brother." Tucker glanced at me. "Isis wasn't able to turn it around?"

"No. She was searching for her husband's body, with the help of Nephthys."

"Ah. The sister felt guilty?"

"Super guilty. Maybe about having sex with her brother/bro-in-law, maybe about triggering Set, maybe both. Either way, interesting tidbit: Isis and Nephthys changed into falcons, or kites, to search for Osiris."

Tucker frowned. "They asked someone to fly them as kites? What if someone let go of the string?"

I giggled. "I thought the same thing. I had to look it up. 'Kites' is another word for falcons. Their cries sound like grief. And falcons are associated with Horus—"

"Horus, the other brother that no one cares about?"

"No. Horus, the next generation. Patience, grasshopper." He laughed. He calls me grasshopper all the time. I patted his knee. I'm less sleazy than the douche. "First thing. They found Osiris's casket. It crashed into a tree near Byblos."

Tucker sighed in recognition. "That's the name of a great restaurant in Montreal. Tori wouldn't share any of her chicken. I still remember that it came with tarragon yogurt and saffron."

Tori's a cool cat (not literally; she's a resident doctor like us) and the artist who made us the card with the Egyptian quotes, but I waved him back to my story. "Byblos was an ancient city in what is now Lebanon."

"Yeah, I know."

"Pretty incredible, right?" I showed him a map I'd loaded up on my phone earlier. "The casket would have had to float all the way from the Nile to the Mediterranean Sea, past what is now Israel, up to Byblos, which is north of what's now Beirut." In other words, a really long way for any bird to fly or casket to float.

Tucker read my mind. "It's a more interesting story that way. So, putting aside probability and p values, Isis found his body."

"Well, first the king and queen of Byblos found the tree that the casket was lodged inside. The tree had taken on the beauty and even the scent of Osiris. The royal couple cut down the tree and used it as a central pillar in the court."

Tucker's nostrils flared. "And that's helpful how?"

"Yeah. Drowned in a casket, crashed into a tree, and cut down as a tree. I thought, *Welp, he's dead x 3*. But actually, he was kind of reborn into the tree."

"Osiris was dead, but the tree absorbed his essence."

I nodded.

Tucker shook his head. "Then the king and queen of Byblos cut it down."

"Right, dead x 3—but born x 4. He's still in that tree, whether it's been cut down or not." I yawned. What a day. "Isis disguises herself as an older woman and makes friends with the—Bybliotic?—queen's handmaidens by the shore. That queen eventually trusts Isis to nursemaid her own sons. Isis decides to make the younger Byblos prince immortal by 'burning away part of his mortality' every night."

"Uh oh."

"Yeah, I don't know what that means, but it must've been bad because the Queen of Byblos catches her and freaks out, whereupon Isis reveals herself as the goddess. The King and Queen beg Isis to spare their lives, and Isis relinquishes them on one condition: she wants that central pillar."

Tucker's mouth twitched between a smile and a frown. "The Osiris tree."

"Exactly. Somehow, that tree gets converted to human form, and Isis and Nephthys embalm his body and carry out funeral rituals. Osiris is considered the very first mummy."

Tucker snapped his fingers. "I read about that!"

"Right. They carry his mummy home and hide it in the marshes of the Nile Delta. Isis needs more ritual herbs, so she sets out, leaving her sister to stand guard—"

"Nuh-uh!"

"Uh huh. Set persuades Nephthys to tell him where Osiris's body is. Then he hacks it up and throws all the pieces into the Nile."

20

SATURDAY

ead x 4.

I woke up in our hotel bed, my head still aching. I hate to admit it, but that's a souvenir from a concussion on the world's worst flight a month ago: occasionally, when head pain skewers me, I wish someone would shoot me in the brainstem and get it over with.

Tucker's legs spasmed. He'd stolen most of the covers, and his sweat smelled like onions. I snagged the top cover, rolled on my back, and tried to sink into sleep.

Something else had woken me up. But what?

Dead x 4. I was dream-musing about super-slayed Osiris. Drowned, smashed into a tree, chopped down as a tree, and dismembered as a mummy. Can't get much deader than that.

I tried turning on each side and even on my stomach while Tucker snored.

Finally, I gave up and checked my phone. Even though I'd turned off notifications, my Spidey sense must have kicked into overdrive. Ten minutes ago, at 5 a.m., I'd received a message from Noeline Momberg.

Dr. Sze, could you please make sure Gizelda Becker gets her red book?

She's not answering her phone. She checked out of her hotel. Her flight's not until Thursday morning.

We're flying to ZA to see a surgeon.

I think she'll like Jaco and Fleur's drawings.

I sent it to your hotel. Many thanks.

The red book. Could this be Mr. Becker's notes?

The notes Gizelda had refused to give me?

If Gizelda had made friends with the Mombergs, maybe she'd let the children draw in the pretty red notebook to distract them from their dad's eye and to cheer them up before their urgent flight.

I jumped into some clothes and popped down to the lobby to present my passport as ID. The elderly desk clerk handed me a palm-sized notebook covered in imitation red leather, and I remembered to tip him.

"Thank you, Madam."

"Did I just miss the woman who brought this? Maybe a whole family of four?" I asked him.

He shook his head. "An Uber-Careem dropped it off, madam."

The Mombergs must have headed straight to the airport. The drop-off would have cost more than the notebook was worth, something their family could ill-afford.

Still, what a break for me.

I shut myself in our bathroom and flipped on the light and fan, my heart already thudding in anticipation. If Gizelda had let kids play with the book, I didn't consider it top secret.

I flipped past the childish pen scrawls inside the front cover, praying that they hadn't obscured anything vital further in.

Gizelda Becker's neat, spare handwriting barely covered two pages. The remaining pages were either blank or filled with more Momberg baby art. She must not have been too thrilled with her father's pearls of wisdom. Still, I pored over the few words:

Osiris

Isis

Set

The eye of Horus

Hathor

golden disc

My heart thrummed. The Becker notes actually made sense to me.

Tucker and I had pieced together the rest of the legend last night before we'd fallen asleep. It goes a little something like this.

Nephthys helps Isis find all the pieces of quadfecta-dead mummy Osiris, except his penis. Some say that a fish ate it. ("Ouch," from Tucker.)

Still, they resurrect 99 percent of Osiris. Isis flies around him in falcon/kite form and miraculously becomes pregnant.

Osiris can't rule without a dick—female leaders like Hatshepsut must've come later—so he descends to rule the underworld.

Isis gives birth in the marshes of the Nile, the same area where she'd hidden Osiris's body. This time, Nephthys keeps her secret. Isis and Osiris's son, Horus, survives and eventually challenges Set for the kingdom.

Nine gods agree that Horus wins, but the sun god can't decide. Horus and Set fight for another 80 years, including one battle where they take the form of hippopotami.

Set always plays dirty. He steals Horus's left eyeball while he's sleeping, and a goddess named Hathor has to restore his vision.

In their final and strangest battle, Set dominates Horus by jacking off between his nephew's legs. In their culture, defiling a man with your jizz ensures victory for Set. Horus is only able to trap his uncle's semen in his hands.

When Horus asks Isis for help, she screams and cuts off his hands, which mitigates the bad juju. She tosses Set's nasty spunk into the marsh. Then she takes a sample of Horus's semen and sprays it on Set's lettuce, which Set eats.

So when Set brags to the gods that he "performed the labor of a male" against Horus, the gods light up Set's sperm to show the proof, only to discover his swimmers in the marsh.

Then, thanks to his mom, Horus summons his semen from Set's

head in the form of a golden solar disk. Horus places that disc on his own head, crowning himself.

Thus *Ma'at,* or cosmic balance, is restored. The right king, or at least his offspring, takes the throne. Plus it sounds like he got his hands back.

Obviously, this legend had spoken to Phillip Becker. He made his daughter take dictation on it during their vacation.

But why?

What was the clue in this legend, if any?

Tucker snored so loudly that I could hear it over the bathroom fan.

My heart leapt as I scanned the next page, trying to make sense of it before he woke up. Yep, call me petty, but I wanted to crush this while Tucker got his Z's.

Cat

☥

Antiquities
Anubis
Bata
Wife
Beer
Flower

Bull

Carnarvon

L 12:15

Wow. Pretty good drawing of a cat. Who knew Gizelda Becker had artistic talent.

The ankh, I recognized. I still had mine in my thigh pouch. I should move it somewhere safer and/or buy a chain for it.

I moved on to Anubis. I remembered his jackal's head, and the fact that he had a role in the underworld. Turned out Anubis was the original god of the dead before Osiris. Some said he was the son of Bastet, the cat-headed god; others believed he was the son of Ra and Nephthys; still more said he was the illegitimate son of Osiris and Nephthys; some melded Anubis and Osiris together.

I started pacing. Quietly. So far, Phillip Becker had seemed to have a predilection for the afterlife. Did he know he was going to die?

I mean, all 87-year-olds should be aware of their mortality. Still.

When I entered "Bata" in my phone, it pointed me to shoes, but my search engine soon spat out the Tale of Two Brothers, Anubis and Bata.

Anubis is the older, married god, and Bata is the younger, hunky brother. Anubis's wife tries to seduce Bata. He refuses. Out of vengeance, she lies to her husband that Bata came on to her and beat her. Enraged, Anubis sets off to kill his younger brother.

Bata prays to Ra, the sun god, who magics up a crocodile-filled lake between the two brothers. With this protection in place, Bata calls out the truth to his brother, and as proof of his sincerity, Bata cuts off his own equipment and throws it in the lake, where it's snapped up by a catfish.

(At this point, I stifled a laugh. What's with all the dick cutting and consumption? Then I tiptoed out of the bathroom and kissed Tucker's knee through the sheet. Sorry. Poor dudes.

My own dude snored on.)

Bata says he's off to the Valley of Cedars. He'll hide his heart in a blossom on top of a tree. If Anubis ever receives a jar of beer that froths over, he should come find his brother.

Anubis believes his bro and returns home to slay his wife.

Eesh.

"Hope?" Tucker rasped.

My heart tried to leap out of my chest as I shoved the notebook under the bed. I took a deep breath. I was lucky to *have* a heart in my chest, unlike Bata. "Yep?"

"What are you doing up?"

I should tell him that I finally got a hold of Becker's notes.

He patted the bed. I climbed in, coaching myself. *Two heads are better than one. We're a team. Tell him.*

His body felt almost too warm against mine. Now the onion smell mixed with his bad breath. I could still hear Tucker's voice in my head, with a faint sneer.

I got this.

We all know you're the "detective doctor," Hope.

Nope.

Nope on all of that.

Technically, I told him the truth. "I'm reading about Anubis and Bata. Can you believe another god got *this* cut off? He did it to himself, though." I slid my hand along Tucker's morning wood, and if he got a little distracted, well. I could always tell him later.

21

"We better not be late," I whispered to Tucker, as we squeezed on the bus after some school kids.

"Worth it," he said back, kissing my cheek.

I laughed and almost told him about the Becker notes right then, but decided to wait until we were alone.

Tucker looked like he was eavesdropping on the middle-aged man who'd let us go in front of him so he could chat on his cell phone. Cell Phone Man wore a white scarf held in place by a black circle of rope, which my mom calls a Lawrence of Arabia headdress, but this one looked authentic.

I raised my eyebrows at Tucker to ask whassup.

He rubbed his thumb and middle fingers together in a way that meant Cell Phone Man was loaded.

Hmph. Well, why would he bother taking a bus then?

Scratch that. I'd take a bus even if I were a billionaire. Except maybe not after a too-close encounter with an IED.

I held onto a pole and used my free hand to look up the headdress. Then I moved on to "Carnarvon," another item from Becker's list.

"We should be okay," said Tucker.

I shoved my phone in my pocket. "What?"

"Wow, are you ever jumpy today." He leaned closer. "Maybe I need to relax you all over again."

I emitted a jagged little laugh, but he didn't notice. He checked his watch. "If we run into too much traffic, maybe we should take an Uber-Careem. Or run."

Crap. The ER chief would hate me even more if I seemed to leave early and come in late. Sweat itched my armpits.

"Why were you reading about Lord Carnarvon?" said Tucker.

"Huh?" I tried to change the subject. "I looked up the headdress. It's called a *ghutra* or *keffiyeh*. I wonder if our ER chief wears one."

"No, he doesn't. Not at work yesterday, anyway. What does that have to do with Lord Carnarvon?"

My jaw tightened. "Um. Well. His name came up." Technically true. Gizelda had said Carnarvon in passing, although it had meant nothing to me until it reappeared on Becker's list. "It turns out that Lord Carnarvon was the man who backed Harold Carter's archeology expeditions."

"And the man who supposedly died from the mummy's curse."

The bus chatter around us shrivelled with Tucker's words. But that must've been my imagination. How many of them even spoke English?

I glanced around at people's averted faces and muttered, "Mummy's curse?"

"Yeah! The curse of the pharaoh!" Tucker thrust his free hand in the air, making the rock and roll sign.

I had to laugh. "Shh. I've heard of that, but so far, all I saw was that Lord Carnarvon married rich and funded Harold Carter's archaeological digs. Carter found the tomb of King Tut."

"Right. And on the day that Howard Carter opened the tomb, on the 29th of November in 1922, a cobra broke into Carter's own home and killed his pet canary."

I shook my head. Did I hear him wrong? "His canary?"

"Yes, a messenger heard the canary cry out before it died. He said it almost sounded human."

"Aww." That poor, tiny, delicate yellow bird. "On the other hand, a canary *would* look like lunch to a cobra."

"Right, but think symbolically. The cobra represents the Egyptian monarchy. That cobra eating Carter's canary looked like retribution for opening the tomb."

"Poor birdie. I'd call that more than symbolic. And didn't you say Lord Carnarvon died too?"

"He died on April fifth, 1923. About four months later. He got a mosquito bite on his left cheek which turned into cellulitis, sepsis, and pneumonia."

I counted up the months as I squeezed against people's knees to allow more riders on the bus. Four months and six days. "Hmm. That's a bit of a time lag."

"Yeah, a bit. Sir Arthur Conan Doyle theorized that Carnarvon could have been killed by 'elementals' that King Tut's priests had sequestered to guard the royal tombs."

I made a mental note to look that up. I hadn't realized Sherlock Holmes's creator had any connection to Egypt. "Did anyone else die?"

Tucker grinned and scanned his phone. "Well, considering that this all happened a century ago, all of them. But you're asking if any of them were felled by the curse sometime close to 1922, right? One man died with a fever on the French Riviera in May 1923. A member of the excavation team was poisoned with arsenic in 1928. Carter's secretary died in 1929—they think someone smothered him."

"Good God!"

The balding businessman in front of me glanced up from his phone to check that I was okay. I gave a pained smile.

Tucker half-hugged me, still eyeing his screen. "It's not that bad. Carter didn't die until 1939. On average, the 25 Europeans who attended the official opening lived a normal lifespan. Lord Carnarvon's daughter held on for another 57 years."

"Right. The timeline is suspect. But if two people in the party were murdered, that seems high."

"Yeah, and check this!"

I nearly laughed at his excitement and translated expression.

Québecois people sometimes yell "Check *ça!*", which rubs off on English Quebecers.

Tucker tapped his phone. "Carter gave his friend, Sir Bruce Ingram, a paperweight made of a *mummified hand.*"

"Ew."

"Wait, there's more! The hand had a bracelet inscribed 'Cursed be he who moves my body. To him shall come fire, water, and pestilence.'"

I stared at him. "And did he get fire, water, and pestilence?"

"Apparently Sir Bruce Ingram's house burned down right after he received the hand. He rebuilt the house, and then it flooded."

"Ugh. Did Ingram end up with pestilence, too?"

"Wikipedia didn't mention it, but he probably had mice. Remember how cats are supposed to be sacred in Egypt because they were so good at killing the mice that ate the grain?"

"Let's stick to one story for now." I sighed. The businessman in front of me popped open his briefcase and tried not to react to either of us. "So the curses probably don't work. And yet, for the rest of the month, I promise I'll stay away from King Tut and mummy hands."

"It's a deal." Tucker smacked a kiss on my cheek, and then gave a low whistle at his phone.

"What is it?"

"Just got a notice. Someone thinks they recognize the guy from the ICU."

The guy with Phillip Becker's cobra bag. We exchanged a long look, and then I murmured in Tucker's ear, "The game is afoot. I have something to tell you later, too."

22

I kept an eye out for the chief as we walked into the ER together at precisely 0800. My turn on the acute side today, and I was looking forward to it, although the number of patients in the hallway made me uneasy.

Anyone stuck in the hallway in Montreal gets a stretcher, at least. In this case, I saw families surrounding patients on chairs. One woman seemed to nurse a baby while she was sitting on the floor.

Rudy greeted Tucker with a complicated handshake that made both of them grin.

"You good?" said Rudy.

"I'm good, man. Ready to rock and roll."

As if on cue, a man's voice cried out behind us, and a woman's voice raised in alarm.

I spun around to watch the door from the waiting room burst open. While a nurse yelled at them in Arabic, the man ported a child into the hallway.

The boy's head bobbed in a way that made me clench my teeth.

Tucker and I rushed to their side. I couldn't follow the language, so I focused on the boy, who looked maybe four. Sand clotted his hair, his nostrils, and lips. His eyes were closed, his body limp. He looked grey under his melanin.

"How old is he?" I asked Rudy, who'd been talking to the grey-haired dad.

"Five years."

I added the age to my pediatric phone app. It automatically calculates the correct medication doses per weight, so I can concentrate on other stuff like the ABC's.

"What happened to him?" I said, eyeballing the Airway and Breathing (A and B). No obvious choking or snoring in dad's arms, but he was breathing fast and shallow, with that odd colour.

Rudy struggled to translate in real time. "He was ... playing underground. We pulled him out of the sand. We thought he might get better, but—"

The dad called out, frantic.

We needed the kid on a stretcher, with oxygen, an IV, a cardiac monitor, and a glucose check to start.

The black-clad woman behind them, probably mom, pointed at a bloody smear on the boy's sandy left ankle. I wasn't sure what to make of that. It looked like the least of his problems.

The grandmother added something I couldn't understand.

"He can't breathe!" A pretty, dark-haired girl, maybe seven, rushed up to my side. "Can you help him?"

"We'll try." I turned to direct them to the resuscitation bay, one of four glass-walled rooms on the right side of the hallway, but Rudy stopped us. "They have to register."

I whipped around to stare at him.

Rudy said, in a flat voice, "Those are the rules. They need to register and pay. Security should have stopped them from coming in."

Two men in dark uniforms nodded back at him from behind the family.

I paused to check the family more carefully. This time, I noticed that the little boy's frayed pants had ripped at the knees. The dad's shaggy hair hung in his eyes. The mom was covered in what I think is called a niqab, with only her eyes showing through cloth that had faded to greyish-black.

These people were poor. They probably couldn't pay for their treatment. Which meant that the boy would die.

I wanted to grab Rudy and yell, "But this is Canada!" We treat life-threatening injuries first and ask questions later.

Except this *wasn't* Canada. We needed to play by Egyptian rules.

"Please. We will pay," his sister piped up in her little voice.

I shuddered. Even at her age, she already knew the game. She knew they needed money to buy her brother's life.

"Good enough for me," said Tucker. "We need a stretcher!" He raised his voice and repeated it in Arabic, using his hands to signal that he wanted the boy to lie down.

Slowly, two women who looked like nurses came forward, spoke to the family, and led them toward trauma bay #2.

Yes! Come on, come on, I mentally urged them as I trailed behind them. We usually run to resuscitate sick kids.

The boy moaned.

Well, at least that bought his Glasgow Coma Scale up another point.

The father barked something, his arms still full of his son, and the mother pulled a wallet out of the dad's back pocket.

One of the women must have been patient registration, because she tried to take Mom with her. Patient reg adds the patient to the record system and takes your health card, or in this case, your credit card or cash. Mom hesitated.

The father jerked his chin at her.

"We'll take care of him!" I called to Mom, and she nodded at me as if she understood.

The little daughter called out something reassuring too, and Mom slowly left her son.

"We need gloves," said Tucker, and I scanned the resus room. Normally they mount racks of gowns, gloves, and masks on walls in the resuscitation bay or just outside, in the hallway.

We did need gloves. Over six percent of the Egyptian population is infected with Hepatitis C, a rate ten times higher than in Canada.

Hep B and HIV are "only" about 1 percent each in Egypt, but yeah. I don't need my liver attacked or my immune system compromised for the rest of my life.

Where could we get gloves? Rudy hadn't followed us in. The remaining nurse quizzed Dad and sister.

Tucker spoke to the nurse, who shook her head and said something curt.

Tucker ran his hand through his hair and turned back to me, pale. "We should have brought our own gloves. We can go buy them at the pharmacy."

"Right now? But he's a code purple!" That's a pre-arrest.

He shook his head. "The patients and Rudy already spotted me yesterday. He said I'd have to get the next box. It's BYOG."

Bring Your Own Gloves. Unreal. "Damn it. The staff doctor covered me yesterday and didn't say anything. I forgot what you said about patients bringing their own cast material."

"Yeah. I was distracted yesterday too." He meant our "detective doctor" fight last night.

No time for that. "We can buy gloves, but not now."

"Agreed. They must have some. We can borrow them and pay them back."

I glanced at the boy. "And he probably doesn't have anything infectious." No one wants to do mouth-to-mouth resuscitation, but when kids are involved, we do.

Tucker raised his eyebrows.

I glanced from the boy's bloody foot to my own intact-looking hands. Should be okay. But no guarantees. I'd assessed a whole bunch of people yesterday. Theoretically, *I* could infect the boy. We both needed protection.

I felt like crying. I pushed that aside. "Well, the rest of the team will be here soon. They'll have gloves. Until then, I'll do the history, and you can translate."

Tucker opened his mouth, but I moved toward the kid, whom the father had laid on the stretcher. Then I realized the kid was unconscious, the dad and grandma probably didn't speak English, and the sister might be seven years old.

Awright. Moving on to physical exam.

"Airway and C-spine," I said to Tucker. The father tried to steady the boy without covering him up from my inspection. "Did he fall and hit his head and neck?"

"He was buried in sand. They had to dig him out," the sister volunteered. "My other brother called us to come get him."

"Okay. We should get a C-spine collar on him in case," I said.

"Does he have any health problems or allergies?" Tucker cut in.

The girl spoke to the dad a bit before she turned back to us. "No."

"Okay. Let's get him some oxygen already," I said. We didn't have any vital signs, but the kid looked "like ass," as one of the St. Joe's nurses would say.

I caught the Cairo nurse's eye and pretended to string nasal prongs up my nose and hook them around my ears.

She shook her head at me, even though she was already wearing gloves.

"He needs oxygen." I mimed a face mask this time and pointed to the oxygen dial mounted on the wall.

Tucker began speaking in a low, calm voice. Maybe because he was a white, male, foreign M.D., or possibly because he spoke Arabic, or all of the above, she crossed to the wall and unwrapped some nasal prongs.

"O2, BP, monitor," I said to Tucker, but there was only one nurse. The hospital could be short-staffed, or holding off until the family paid. Or both.

"I can do the monitor," said Tucker.

He spoke to the dad, asking permission before lifting the boy's shirt.

"It's better if you leave it for someone with gloves," I said.

"Hope." Tucker's lips pressed together.

"I'm sorry, but it is." I glanced at Tucker's abdomen, knowing the exact surgical scars hidden by his shirt.

Tucker loathed when I brought that up. He shook his head at me and reached for the electrodes.

"It's just ... be careful. I love you," I added, under my breath.

Tucker's face flashed between anger and pleasure. He closed his eyes in acknowledgement.

I'd never said ILY over a resuscitation before. I was losing it.

I turned back to the boy and located an adult-sized oxygen saturation probe that fell off the end of his finger. We needed to clip one on his ear, or tape one to his fingertip.

Meanwhile, the nurse slowly, slowly attached the cardiac leads to stickers on the boy's bare chest, revealing a sinus tachycardia at 179. Kids can go fast, but this was pretty fast. We still didn't have a blood pressure.

"Glucose," said Tucker.

Yep. Kids (well, more infants) can go hypoglycemic during a resuscitation. Better keep an eye on all his electrolytes.

With a rip of Velcro, the nurse attached a blood pressure cuff to the boy's arm, which slid down to his elbow. She shook her head.

Right. This wasn't a pediatric hospital. We'd have to approximate his BP by taking his carotid, femoral, and radial pulses. If we could touch him.

"What is going on here?" called a dark-skinned man in a lab coat, surrounded by a bevy of med students and residents. He glared at me and Tucker, but the important part was that he spoke English and he probably had gloves.

The nurse took a step back. She wanted no part of this.

"I have a five-year-old who was buried in sand and at least partially suffocated," I said, not turning a hair. As far as I'm concerned, a sick kid trumps everything. "You can see he's tachycardic, we need a C-spine collar, a pediatric BP cuff, a glucose, and a full set of labs. He needs a CT head and C spine with a decreased level of consciousness, GCS—"

"Who are you?" The doctor barely glanced at the child. His gaze lodged on my left ear.

"I'm Dr. Hope Sze, a resident doctor from Canada."

He jerked a thumb at the doorway.

He couldn't kick me out. I glanced at a second nurse frozen in the doorway, with a glucometer in her hand.

He's joking, right?

She wouldn't make eye contact with me, but after a beat, she moved aside to let me through, the beige curtain swaying behind her.

Tucker opened his mouth. "Dr. Sharif—"

Damn it. Perfect way to meet the Chief of ER: him booting me out of a pediatric resus.

"Please, Dr. Sharif," I added quietly.

Medicine is a hierarchy. As the new female Canadian resident doctor in the Middle East who couldn't speak Arabic and had no gloves, I could hardly claim status as an essential member of the resuscitation team.

Tucker tried again. "Dr. Sharif, Dr. Sze and I can tell you all about this previously healthy five-year-old boy, no medications, no allergies—"

Dr. Sharif shook his head. "Get her out of here. Now. Has this patient been registered?" he asked, as a third woman in a white head scarf urged me and Tucker toward the door, away from the boy.

Uh oh. If they stopped the resus to get official documents and payment, this kid could die.

"At least get the glucose," I pleaded with the second nurse, as we glided past her and her glucometer in the doorway. "If it ends up being hypoglycaemia, we could treat that."

"He's seizing!" a man shouted, and then someone ripped the beige curtains closed, cutting us off.

23

"WTF," said Tucker.

"I know." I'd never listened to a code from behind a curtain before. Doesn't get any worse than that.

"WT *actual* F," he bit out, hands fisted. He clearly wanted to punch someone.

"You want to run down to the pharmacy for gloves so we can try to get back in there?" I'd wait outside on the infinitesimal chance that Dr. Sharif pulled me back in, since I was the one doing acute care today.

The curtain shifted, and at least four learners left resus, including Rudy. Bad sign. Tucker crossed toward them before Rudy shook his head.

Tucker retreated.

"We're all persona non grata?" I reached for my phone. "Isabelle keeps saying how important we are. Maybe we should get Sarquet Industries to throw their weight around here." I pressed the phone icon, and my phone began to purr.

"Hope," said Tucker.

"You want Youssef? I feel like we should bring in the biggest guns from the get go, but I'm willing to use him as a plan B."

Tucker touched my wrist as Isabelle's liquid voice poured into my ear. "Hello, darling. How are you?"

"Hi Isabelle, not good. We've got a few issues. One of the patients can't pay, but this is a life and death situation."

"Oh, I'm so sorry to hear that. They should speak to the billing department and work out an arrangement."

"Isabelle." I made a conscious effort to slow down and speak clearly, since Tucker has accused me of mumbling. I couldn't mess this up. "Did you hear me? This is *life and death*. As we speak."

"Yes, that's tragic. I sincerely hope they can work something out. Is everything else to your satisfaction?"

I pulled the phone away from my ear to stare at it, as if that would force her to give me a different answer. Tucker was already on his phone too, so he couldn't help. I retreated toward the doctors' lounge. "I can't provide good medical care by withholding it from people who don't have the money."

She sighed. "Oh my goodness, you have a beautiful heart. I'm sure so many people will be inspired by your attitude."

Huh? After a moment, I collected myself enough to say, "We don't need an inspiring attitude. This patient needs *money* for *medical care.*"

"I find it refreshing. I really do. So ... youthful."

I exhaled on a count of four and tried again. "Isabelle, I know that Sarquet Industries has considerable financial resources. If this family can't cover the hospital bill, is it possible that your company might do it? It would be excellent publicity."

"Darling, that's so thoughtful of you. You think so highly of Sarquet Industries. We appreciate you thinking of us, we really do."

I shook my phone instead of screaming. Tucker didn't even look up from his own phone, and I made a superhuman effort to keep it profesh. "Isabelle, is there any chance Sarquet Industries will pay for this medical care and save someone's life?"

"Of course I can ask, but I must warn you not to get your hopes up. After all, it's a slippery slope. There are so many people in need. We couldn't possibly look after all of them."

My throat tightened. "If Tucker and I left, you'd have more money for charity work."

"Dr. Sze!" For the first time, she sounded genuinely alarmed. "Please don't think that way. Your travel and accommodations are not part of—" She bit off her words.

"Part of what?"

"They come from a different budget. At any rate, both of you hardly cost anything. We have connections in the travel industry, and tourist numbers have decreased since 2011. It's our pleasure and our honour to welcome you."

"Isabelle, I can't sit here as some sort of mascot. I want to make real change, or I might as well go home."

"No, please don't, Dr. Sze! I will discuss this. Send me the patient's billing details, with his or her permission, and I'll see if I can make some sort of exception, this time and this time only. Is that clear?"

"Yes. Thank you, Isabelle."

"You're welcome, Dr. Sze." She hung up.

My heart galloped as fast as the little boy's. I'd gotten what I wanted, but why? How?

I rolled my shoulders back and turned toward resus. The little girl rushed up to me, her dark hair swinging and her small, brown face alight. "Can you come back and help my brother?"

"Hi, sweetie. I would love to." I glanced up past her at the grand-mother, who'd followed quietly in her black robes. "We need gloves and, uh, the chief of the emergency department, Dr. Sharif, has taken over his care right now. What's your brother's name?"

"Hadi."

"That's a great name," said Tucker, joining us and smiling down at her. "A strong name."

"You think so?" said the girl.

"Absolutely," said Tucker. "I wish I had a name like that. My real first name is John. In English, it's also slang for a toilet."

The little girl covered her mouth. The grandmother looked like she was trying not to laugh at their comical expressions. I willed

Tucker not to tell them that it's also slang for the guys who hire prostitutes.

"So many people are named John. It's boring. So, starting around when I was your age, I told my friends, 'I'm Tucker.' Do you think you could call me that?"

The girl glanced at me, then back at Tucker. "But you're a doctor?"

"Sure, you can call me Dr. Tucker if you want. What's your name?"

"Amal," she said.

"Oh, like the lawyer who married George Clooney!" I exclaimed.

Tucker, Amal, and even the grandmother blinked at me.

"Sorry, maybe George Clooney's not popular in Egypt," I said.

"We're from Yemen, but we know about Amal Clooney. She's the barrister!" said the girl.

"Yes, she argued on behalf of the three Al-Jazeera journalists, including the Canadian, Mohamed Fahmy," said Tucker, offering her a high five.

Amal smacked his hand enthusiastically while I secretly wished I could Google that. How embarrassing when a kid knows more about world politics than you do.

"You speak very good English," said Tucker, which is a phrase I heard too often from white people who assumed it was my second language.

"My big brother taught me. We have to make money," Amal informed Tucker gravely. "My brothers can go out and work, but not me."

"Nowadays, women work too," I said.

Amal shook her head. "Not us."

"We consider it work if you cook and clean and raise children too." I included the grandmother in my smile, and I thought I saw her eyes crinkle through the window of the niqab.

"But we need money for Hadi," said Amal.

"I agree. I'm asking our friends if they'll donate money from Canada for him," said Tucker, waving his phone.

"Are there rules about crowdfunding for patients?" I whispered.

He shrugged.

Great.

"Oh, Dr. Tucker, you think they might?" Amal jumped up and all but clapped her little hands.

"They might. We'll try."

Amal began explaining it to her grandmother, interrupting herself to pepper Tucker with questions.

When she simmered down, I said, "Amal, I have some questions for your parents. There may be a company that can help pay for Hadi's treatment, but I need their permission to send them your brother's bill. Could you bring me to them?"

Amal clapped in excitement and translated for her grandmother before taking my hand with her cool, little fingers. "Yes. Let's go. We need to help my brother. Help him against the scorpion."

24

"The scorpion?" I repeated, as we motored toward the nursing station. "You think he was bitten by a scorpion?"

She nodded her head, turning her gorgeous brown eyes on me as her fingers tightened on mine. "Hadi had nightmares about them. They like dark places, you know. He used to cry and shake and say, 'Don't make me go down there!' But he had to. And now he's dead."

"He's not dead!" I exclaimed. "At least he wasn't when we left. Let's go check on him now."

"That's true. And Amal, scorpions sting instead of biting," Tucker said, coming up behind us with the grandmother.

Oops. I was the one who'd said bitten. I flushed and didn't realize I'd squeezed Amal's hand too hard until she squeaked and pulled it away.

Tucker paused in front of cubicle number 5. "They use their tails instead of their mouths. They're arachnids, like spiders. Do you really think a scorpion stung him?"

Her tiny chin nodded up and down as she fell into step with him and her grandmother instead. "His nightmare came true."

Tucker and I exchanged a look. Muhamed had told me scorpions don't live in Cairo. What was fact vs. fancy in a seven-year-old's brain?

"We should ask the team if it's a possibility," I murmured, as nurses bustled around us and a patient in the hall yelled.

Tucker didn't answer. We both knew that if anyone was going to ask Dr. Sharif about scorpions, it would be him, since the chief somehow couldn't stand me. And if Tucker reported a scorpion sting based on a seven-year-old's report of a five-year-old's nightmare, we'd get laughed out of the department.

Tucker smiled at Amal. "I'll take a look at his ankle. That's what your mom was pointing at. Then I'll ask your dad."

I recalled that smear of blood on his miniature ankle. A scorpion sting? Or something else?

All four of us paused in front of trauma bay #2's beige curtain.

A gaunt man called out to us from a chair on the left. He only wore pants and sandals, so I got a good view of his ribs jutting out of his chest.

"He looks sick," said Amal. "When you die, they weigh your heart with a feather."

Uh oh. I'd heard of this Egyptian legend, too. "They used to believe that a long time ago," I said.

Amal nodded. "If your heart is heavier than the feather, they throw your heart to a monster who eats it. And then you disappear!"

"We don't believe in monsters. We believe in science and medicine to help your brother," Tucker told her. "Let me go in and talk to the other doctors. I'll see what I can find out."

"Great. Thanks, Dr. Tucker. I'll see if other patients need help, too." I turned to Amal. "When your parents come out, I have to talk to them about the bill, okay? In case the company can help you pay."

She beamed. "Thank you, doctors!"

"You're welcome."

Luckily, I'd been officially assigned to another ER doctor, not Dr. Sharif, but Dr. Kyrollos. She was female, maybe 55, stocky, and no-nonsense in a white coat and bright red lipstick. No head scarf.

"I heard about you," Dr. Kyrollos told me, unsmiling.

Behind her, a thin, dark male doctor laughed and added something that sounded like "sarudi."

"Sa-Rudy?" I repeated. "You want to talk to Dr. Rudy?"

Dr. Kyrollos's spine straightened, and she snapped at that doctor in Arabic. He turned away, irritated.

Yet another mystery. One I couldn't solve as I picked up my next chart, a pedestrian who'd been hit by a car and had an open tib-fib fracture. Then a frail woman in severe renal failure who couldn't afford dialysis. The gaunt man in the hallway thought ghosts were talking to him.

So I was relieved to spot Hadi an hour later, strapped to a stretcher and ready for transfer to a pediatric hospital.

Even if Hadi still seemed unconscious.

25

"Hadi nearly suffocated," said Tucker that night, in our hotel. "The sand must have caved in on him."

My guy's serious face and tone contrasted with his spiky post-shower hair, wilder than Albert Einstein's.

I sat on on our bed and set two plastic forks on top of our Styrofoam box of day-old koshary, which balanced on the bedspread between us. "I saw the sand on him. But why was he underground?"

"I don't know." Tucker tossed an old paperback, *The Murder of Roger Ackroyd,* onto his bedside table before he folded his legs to sit across from me on the bed. "I asked the mom and dad a few times, in Arabic, until the rest of the team told me to leave it alone."

"They were probably more worried about his neuro status," I agreed. "Did they end up stabilizing him?"

"I only got a quick look at him and the monitor. He was maintaining his O2 sat with nasal prongs at the time, and his BP was stable. Then they asked me to go to the ambulatory side, so I don't know any more than you do."

We both stared at the closed box of koshary. Neither of us had worked up an appetite yet. At the hospital, I'd barely managed to scribble down my Egyptian phone number and hand it to the grand-mother before the paramedics came for Hadi.

No one had called me. For all I knew, Isabelle would keep blowing me off, and the family could not afford pediatric ICU care.

"What do you think of this elective so far?" I said.

Tucker flashed a smile at me. "Definitely the weirdest. And that's saying a lot with you around"

"Did you get any word on a scorpion, or what made the mark on his ankle?"

Tucker picked up his fork and drummed it against his palm. "I didn't want to ask and look even more stupid."

"Understood." I took a deep breath. This might be a good time to tell him about the Becker notes. *You're not stupid. We got clues!* I asked him another question first. "Hey, this is random, but does it mean anything if you add 'sa' onto someone's name? Like 'sa-hope' or 'sa-tucker'? Like in Japan, you'd say Hope-san out of respect?"

He raised his eyebrows. "Not that I've ever heard. Why?"

"Oh, just another niggly thing. On the acute side, a guy said 'saru-di.' I wondered if he was talking about Rudy."

Tucker burst out laughing so hard that I held down the Styrofoam box and utensils to make sure everything didn't fall off the bed. He chortled, "Hope! Sarudi just means Saudi. As in, Saudi Arabian."

"Well, how am I supposed to know that? Saudi is shorter than Sarudi."

Tucker shrugged, his shoulders still shaking. "Sorry. I guess I needed a laugh."

Mmph. I grabbed my fork and threw open the koshary lid for something to do.

Then I inhaled. The tomato sauce still smelled good. Ali knew what he was doing.

"Well, even if the medicine sucks, I got a lead on identifying the guy with the cobra bag," said Tucker.

"How on earth did you find that guy? Seems impossible in a city of 10 million people—double that if you include the suburbs."

Tucker waggled his eyebrows and gestured at the koshary. "Ladies first."

I winked at him and managed to balance some rice, macaroni, and lentils on my fork, but spilled them when I speared some fried onions. I shoved what I could in my mouth and said around that, "Not bad!"

Tucker chewed and grinned. "Yeah, I think there's some vinegar in the sauce. Anyway, for the cobra guy, I posted it on Facebook and Twitter and Instagram and Reddit and Discord and anywhere else. Kevin helped too."

"My *little brother* helped you from Canada?"

"Yeah. Him, Reza, Tori, Mireille, anyone. It doesn't matter, as long as you're boosting the signal. And I had a secret weapon."

"A billion friends?"

"Yes! Including Rudy, Maryam and Ali. The Mombergs retweeted it. The dad's recovered part of the vision in his eye, by the way, so that's promising."

"Phew."

"I even asked Isabelle and Youssef, but they didn't respond."

I grabbed my water from the bedside table and sipped it to clear a chick pea from my throat. "So basically you hit up everyone you've ever met?"

"Exactly! Then I went through all the suggestions and narrowed it down to two." He wiped his hands on a napkin so he could show me a photo.

I made a face. "That guy looks a bit fatter."

"And ten years older. But this one ... " He moved to the next shot.

I sucked in my breath as I stared at the screen.

"Looks juuuuuust right," Tucker drawled.

I dropped my fork back into the styrofoam box we shared. "Who is he?"

"According to LinkedIn, Mr. Abdallah Hussein is an Egyptologist and private consultant who has worked for several museums. I messaged him."

"Hold up. He works for museums? Like the one that they tried to bomb on Wednesday?"

Tucker shook his head, shut the box of koshary, and got up to set it in the fridge. "His c.v. isn't up to date, so I'm not sure. In the past ten years, he's had contracts at both the Museum of Egyptian Antiquities, which is in downtown Cairo, and the new one. That's the Grand Egyptian Museum, in Giza, near the Pyramids. The one with the IED."

"And that's the one Phillip Becker was trying to visit. So maybe the treasure is in the Grand Egyptian Museum, or the key to it is in that cobra bag."

"That's what I think, too. Occam's Razor: it's the simplest explanation. The problem is proving any of it."

I shook my head. "It's still amazing! So do you have any contact info for Mr. Abdallah Hussein? Maybe through his publications?" Lead authors list their e-mails.

"Nah. His last publication was four years ago, and he wasn't the lead author. But he does have a Twitter account, @OsirisPhD." Tucker showed it to me.

The photo definitely still looked like the same guy, although his hair was a little longer and his face fuller. However, there was a bigger problem. "This page is in Arabic."

"Ta dah!" Tucker clicked and translated it into English.

I scrolled through the posts. Lots of them were retweets (RT), reposting other people's articles:

RT: 10 Plagues of Egypt. Legend or reality?

I admired his RT'd photo of a green crystal called dioptase which had occasionally been mistaken for emeralds in ancient times. He also retweeted the occasional cat video. He posted one pic of his family. The littlest kid was maybe two.

Occasionally, he answered people's questions, mostly in English:

Yes, Osiris death in Nile is basis for belief that drowning in Nile is sacred.

No, Isis was nursemaid for the sons of the king and queen of Byblos. Isis bathes younger son in fire, trying to make him immortal.

Someone named @meinklaus replied to that one: *lol #IsisFail*

I rolled my eyes. I avoided Twitter because of trolls. Still, I pointed out the obvious. "@OsirisPhD mostly talks about Egyptian history, especially Osiris and Horus." I shot Tucker a look. "Like Phillip Becker."

Tucker lifted one shoulder. "Not so unusual in an Egyptologist, maybe, but between that and the cobra bag, he's definitely a person of interest."

"If he's at the museum, you think it's safe for us to go visit him? After the IED?"

Tucker nodded firmly as he stretched back on the bed with me. "They've stepped up security. Like I said, they don't want to lose any more tourists. I told him we could treat him to dinner somewhere else, too. His choice."

Comforting thought. Oh, well. Abdallah Hussein hadn't even answered Tucker's messages yet.

Tucker swung his legs out and knocked *The Murder of Roger Ackroyd* to the ground. As he picked it up, he said, "I've barely gotten to read that thing. My mom gave it to me. You know what's weird, though? It talks about Rikki-tikki-tavi."

I pressed my lips together. "You're kidding."

"Seriously. Right near the beginning."

I flipped to a dog-eared page. The narrator says his sister is so curious, she's like a mongoose. He thinks she should adopt the mongoose family motto, "Go and find out."

I shook my head. "It's probably a coincidence that your mom gave us a book with a mongoose. You know what it's called when you see something once, and then it seems to appear everywhere, just because you're looking for it?"

"Right. Total Baader-Meinhof Phenomenon."

Anyway. I took a deep breath. *Time to put up or shut up, Hope.* "I've got some news, too. I have the notes Gizelda Becker made for her dad."

"What? *How?* Did you find anything?"

"Sort of." I brandished the red notebook.

"That's awesome! You're fantastic!"

I beamed as I handed it to him. It actually felt good to relinquish it. While he perused the little red book, I finished researching the story of Anubis and Bata in more detail online.

To recap: Anubis kills his faithless wife (wah) and Bata heads off to what is now Lebanon to build a beautiful home.

There, the god Khnum takes pity on Bata and creates the world's most gorgeous woman for him, although Khnum predicts that she will die by the sword.

Bata adores his Heavenly Wife. That's my name for her, since she was created by a god and doesn't seem to have an official moniker. Unfortunately, a) Bata's also missing some crucial equipment to satisfy her, and b) the heavenliness attracts the ocean, so Bata warns her to stay away. Nevertheless, Heavenly Wife heads to the ocean waves, which leap up and pursue her on land. She manages to escape, leaving behind a lock of hair.

That divine hair winds up on the pharaoh's shores, and it smells so irresistible that the pharaoh himself falls for her. Heavenly Wife marries the pharaoh and asks the ruler to cut down Bata's heart tree, which kills him.

I couldn't resist summarizing and continuing the story for Tucker. "Back in Egypt, Anubis's beer ferments. He makes his way to the Valley of Cedars and finds Bata's body in bed. After searching for almost four years, Anubis comes upon a flower that is, upon closer inspection, his brother's shrivelled heart. He places it inside a cup of water. Eventually, the heart drinks its fill and begins to beat once more. Anubis places it in his brother's chest, and Bata returns to life."

"Whew," said Tucker. "Did he get his penis back, too?"

I patted his hand. Always about the peen. "No, but then Bata turns into a bull. And the bull is the symbol of the pharaoh, so the pharaoh's stoked to have such a majestic symbol show up at his palace, certifying him as a divine ruler. Bata the bull lets his wife know who he is, and she in turn asks the pharaoh to kill the bull and feed her his liver."

"Ugh. Shades of Snow White."

"Right. Except this time, there's no merciful hunter. They really do kill the bull."

"And she eats the liver?"

"Presumably. But as they're carrying his dead body into the chamber, Bata the bull shakes his head. Two drops of blood fly on either side of the threshold, and two Persea trees grow."

Tucker made his way to my side of the bed so he could circle his arms around me and rest his chin on my head. "Those trees are Bata, reincarnated?"

"Right-o."

"And he tells the queen who he is again?"

"Of course. Then she asks the pharaoh to cut down the trees and make them into furniture."

"So he becomes a picnic table?"

"Two benches, but yeah. Still, this time she's watching them cut the trees down, and a splinter enters her mouth, making her pregnant."

Tucker snorted. "That's not how it works."

"It does in legend. The newborn baby is Bata himself. So after the pharaoh dies, Bata becomes the king and the god, and denounces his wife. She dies by the sword, like the prophecy predicted."

He grimaced.

"Exactly. We're supposed to concentrate on Bata, the king-god and rightful ruler of the world, who summons his brother and appoints Anubis as one of his muckety-mucks. So now the brothers are reunited."

Tucker ruffled my hair sympathetically. "The wicked women have been decapitated, and all is well."

I sighed. "That's my big problem with it. They blame the women, and I'm not saying they're saints, but the guys could have saved themselves so much grief. I mean, if Bata hadn't cut off his own dick, then maybe his wife would have stayed with him in the first place."

"Harsh."

"Yeah, but she doesn't want to be on house arrest. She wants fresh air. So then the ocean attacks her. And it's not her fault that the gods made her with super-strong smelling hair. Not that it justifies her repeatedly having her husband killed. Ahh, everyone's awful in this story. The only one who doesn't kill anybody is Bata."

Tucker lifted me into his lap and kissed my neck, distracting me. "You're the most gorgeous woman in the world. Please don't have me killed."

I wound my fingers through his hair. "Please don't have me decapitated."

"Deal."

I had to giggle. "Who said romance was dead." I kissed him once, twice, and sighed. "We should talk about Becker's notes. Figure out why he brought up two similar legends."

"Kings getting kicked off their thrones."

"Guys missing this." My hand headed south.

Tucker spread his legs to allow more access. "Treacherous women."

"Isis isn't treacherous! She's more faithful than Penelope!" That part of *The Odyssey* always annoyed me: ever-dependable Penelope, fighting off suitors, while Odysseus screws around.

"But Anubis and Bata both had bad wives." He pressed against my hand. "Nephthys kept going back and forth"—he enacted the back and forth motion, his voice deepening—"on helping her sister and helping her brother-husband."

I wrapped my fingers around the main event. "Well, does that make Nephthys a good sister or a good sister-wife? She kind of took turns."

"In the end, everything turned out all right," said Tucker, pushing me back on the bed and climbing on top of me.

I linked my ankles behind his back and drew his head down for another kiss. "Better than all right."

Then we did our level (and occasionally vertical) best to banish all thoughts of severed penises and women dying by the sword.

I sank into sleep afterward.

Never heard my phone.

26

P*lease doctor*
     help hadi
          I woke up to a dozen texts and phone messages.
we need $$$$$
can u help us?

Some of the texts were photos from the ICU. The little boy looked frail. Intubated. Eyes closed and taped (to prevent corneal abrasions. This hospital knew what it was doing).

But it was not a good sign.

I called back before I was fully awake, before I woke up Tucker, before I peed or brushed my teeth.

The phone rang and rang. No one picked up.

I threw off the warm covers and paced the tiny hotel room, glancing at the time (4:17 a.m.).

I didn't understand the Arabic voice message, but I spoke after the beep. "Sorry, Amal, I didn't see these until now. I'm trying to help. Where are you? What hospital? Call me back."

I checked my e-mail. Nothing from Isabelle.

On the other hand, Amal's parents hadn't sent me the bill. Isabelle had nothing to work with, even if she wanted to, on the weekend. I brought up the voice messages. Two from Amal, with her tiny voice saying the same thing. *We need money.*

Tucker sat up in bed, his hair askew, his voice rough with sleep, but alert. "What is it?"

I showed him my phone. Watched him scroll through ten more pleas. He handed it back to me.

"Did she message you?" I asked.

He reached for his phone on his bedside table. "No. But I didn't give her my number. Let me see how much my crowdfunder got, though."

Time to pace some more. Limited foot space, but I could circle the bed to the window, walk the small hallway to the door, and back to the window. Again and again.

Finally, Tucker said, "It's $139."

It took me a second to dig up an encouraging thought. "That's good. The first hundred is the hardest."

"The first hundred was from me."

"Well. All our friends are poor students. And maybe asleep. My parents will contribute. Hell, I'll put some in. Sorry I hadn't gotten around to it."

"This sucks." A bitter smile slashed across his face. "I'm poor, and I hate it."

"Tucker. You'll graduate in 18 months and start making money."

He shook his head. "You're doing the emerg year. That's another year of tuition and crap pay. And you know how much I owe on student loans and line of credit?"

I tensed. We'd never talked about money, and suddenly, I didn't want to.

"Over $275,000. I have to start paying that back the minute I graduate. And it's not just me. My sisters need tuition too."

I licked my lips. "You're a good brother."

"I'm a month behind after 14/11." He never brought up the hostage taking. I sucked in my breath before he went on, "And you know how much money L.A. cost me?"

I'd asked him once. He'd never answered. He'd told me not to worry about it.

He half-laughed instead of answering now. "Plus we're getting married. That's a wedding. And kids? You want kids, right?"

"Yes. But you know I'll earn money, too, and I don't have as much debt." My parents were saving up for Kevin's tuition. I'd help with that if I could, though.

"You're in the red. We want to have kids before we're 35, right? Which means one or both of us on parental leave, unless we want someone else to raise our kids. It's not like I started working when I was 22. We're fucked. I *hate* not being able to help Hadi."

"Yeah, but we are helping Hadi. We got him into resus and into a pediatric hospital. I asked Isabelle to look at his bills. You're doing the crowdfunding. And—" I hesitated. Tucker might hate me. Oh, what the hell. I'd say it anyway. "—I'm worried that Amal keeps asking me for money."

Tucker gazed at me from the window side of the bed while I stood on the bathroom side, one king-sized comforter between us.

I forced the words out of my throat. "She's not asking for our medical expertise. She wants money."

"Well, they're at a pediatric hospital now. They have medical expertise. That's not the issue."

"Right. So the one thing she wants from us is cash. She hasn't sent me a bill to forward to Isabelle. I'm not in Hadi's circle of care. I don't even know what hospital he's in. He didn't have any obvious injuries with us except he was unresponsive. She sent photos, but I can't be sure it's the same kid. Meanwhile, the cutest little girl keeps asking us for cash."

"Hope."

I wasn't sure what to make of his voice. Disapproval? Disappointment? Dis-something, anyway. "Sorry if I seem too suspicious, but the whole thing is strange. Amal says a scorpion bit him, but Muhamed told me there aren't scorpions in the city. We know that Hadi was buried in sand, but no one will tell us how it happened."

"Babe. We're both exhausted. Maybe you should come back to

bed and sleep on it. We're not going to raise more money at four in the morning."

"It's 10:30 p.m. back home. The whole thing stinks, Tucker. Why'd we get a free trip to Egypt when a third of their own young people are unemployed? Was the IED a coincidence, or did someone kill Phillip Becker on purpose? Was Becker ranting, or did he actually keep treasure in the cobra bag that his daughter gave away?"

Tucker climbed over the bed and sat with his legs dangling on my side, but didn't try to touch me. "Okay. We can do something about the last part. We have today off. I was going to take you to the Pyramids, but we can try to find Abdallah Hussein instead."

"You know where he is?"

"He tweeted a photo from El-Malek Fouad yesterday, and he was at the Grand Egyptian Museum last week."

I sighed. "So we're playing Where's Waldo in a city of 20 million people? I guess of those two, I'll pick the GEM, since that's where Phillip Becker was headed. Also, I have no idea where the first one is."

"Perfect. Let me set that up. And you sleep, okay?"

"I can't sleep."

"Just try, babe."

I attempted to meditate to make him feel better. I lay down, breathing in and out for what seemed like an hour. Our friend Tori said she liked to inhale while thinking the word "Space" and exhale on "Freedom."

Maybe it worked, because I could've sworn I'd barely closed my eyes when Tucker made a choking noise.

"What is it?"

"He—he DM'd me."

"Who?" Maybe Rudy would direct message him in the wee hours of the morning.

"Abdallah Hussein. He wants to meet us. Now."

27

"What's up with all the water?" was the first thing I said when the hotel doors opened, revealing dripping grey skies and, more importantly, water up to the hubcaps of the poor vehicles splashing through the streets.

"Not good, miss," said one of the hotel doormen, a younger man with a round face.

That was an understatement. I'd sort of gotten used to the road as a shallow stream, but it had grown so high that now I could detect murky waves of water on the sidewalk too. "Don't the storm drains work?"

"Sorry, miss."

Tucker held up his phone. "Says here that their sewage, drainage systems, and infrastructure are 'dilapidated,' and that the situation is even worse outside of Cairo, especially in the poorer areas.'"

"What, exactly, does that mean?"

"Flooding," said Tucker.

We met each other's eyes.

"I guess we could cancel our meeting," I said.

But I knew neither of us would renege on face time with Abdallah

Hussein, even though we seemed to have waded into the origin story of the phrase "come hell or high water."

"Let me see if he'll meet us closer to our hotel," said Tucker, texting on his phone. "He was hoping we'd go to El-Malek Fouad."

"Where the heck is that, anyway?"

"Southwest of Giza. He said it was important. He had something to show us."

"Could you send me the name of that place? I have no idea how to spell it."

He texted it to me. I should've mapped our destination before heading off before dawn to God knows where. I used to rely on Ryan to tow me around, depending on his excellent sense of direction, but I was in Egypt with another man, for heaven's sake. Time to woman up.

I checked the map and shook my head. "Way too far and too dangerous."

"I'm trying to convince him of that right now."

"We might be able to meet him halfway. At the GEM, maybe."

"Maybe."

Tucker got him on the line, made pleasantries, and put him on speakerphone in time for Abdallah to say, "I don't know if I can travel to the city. I am very busy."

Busy, hell. At 5 a.m. on a Sunday? Irritation zapped through me. Try working in an emergency room with an unconscious kid after a transatlantic fight and an IED, and tell me you're busy.

Tucker uttered a soothing, "I'm sure. Dr. Sze and I appreciate your time and expertise."

Abdallah's voice warmed up. "Does that mean you will be able to contribute for my time?"

"Excuse me?" I said before I could stop myself. As Apu used to say on The Simpsons, *What has been implied here?*

"I work as a consultant and have established rates for my time. I'm asking if you and Dr. Tucker are able to compensate me for this visit, including travel."

Damn it. He wanted a bribe. From poor students.

Tucker snatched the phone toward his ear. I reached for it, but he walked away from me, shovelling charm. "Mr. Hussein. This is Dr. Tucker, I'm sure we can figure something out to our mutual convenience. We could treat you to a meal."

"No, I require more substantial compensation for my time," I clearly heard him say through the speakerphone.

The hotel lobby guy watched Tucker move to the edge of the overhang, toward the cars sloshing their way through the water.

I followed Tucker and called out, "How do we know you have anything that we want to hear?"

"You want to know about the bag."

The cobra bag. He was promising to tell us what was in the cobra bag. I decided to push a step further.

"Will you give us the bag?" I'd travel for that.

"Just a second, Hope." Tucker pressed the buttons, moving it off speakerphone and talking to Abdallah in a lower tone before telling me, "Good news. He agreed to a closer meeting place."

"With the bag? For how much?" I eyed the nascent river in the street.

"He wouldn't commit. Just said he'll meet up and we'll 'discuss.'"

"He wants more money."

Tucker grimaced. "I'll stop by a bank machine on the way."

"Tucker, this is blackmail. Or extortion. Something. Should we talk to the police and be done with it?"

After a long minute, while we watched the rain drip off the overhang, and we declined an umbrella from the hotel lobby guy, Tucker said, "I've heard the police want bribes, too. Sometimes you have to pay them just to open a complaint."

I sighed. "Plus what we saw on our first day at the hospital." I could still picture that poor doctor with the fractured nose and the crooked silver glasses.

"Yup."

Everyone here had a hand out. I understood why, but not how I'd fix their problem with my sad line of credit. "We can't go to the middle of nowhere, walk up to him, and say, 'Hey, we're rich tourists, take everything.'"

Tucker thought about it. "We need backup. I'll text everyone here where we're going and who we're meeting."

"They're sleeping, and he wants to meet us before they read their messages. All they'll know is where to search for our dead bodies afterward."

"We're meeting in a public place. Abdul Munir Riad Square. You remember the place where we first changed buses, near the Hotel of Horus?"

"Sort of. I remember the IED better."

We stared at each other. Finally, he said, "I really want to solve this, Hope. I don't think he's dangerous. Egypt is capitalistic, that's all. Rudy explained it to me. They usually won't mug you or steal your stuff. They look you in the eye. They want to work for money and get paid. They hustle, they may harass you, but it's not violent."

I pinched the bridge of my nose. "An IED is more than a hustle, Tucker. I can't stop you?"

He shook his head. "I'm going, Hope. I'm texting our friends as backup, and I'm heading. You can stay here. Maybe that's better anyway."

"Are you nuts?"

Like I'd let my fiancé meet an informant alone. Even if it meant suicide for both of us. I texted my own crew: Kevin, my parents, Grandma, Tori, and even though he'd blocked me, Ryan. *Hi. Heading to Abdul Munir Riad Square. Thinking of you.* "Let's go."

We arrived ten minutes early, in front of a yellow and blue bus terminal sign still showing the same happy bearded dude. I twitched. The last time I saw this sign, we'd run into an IED.

A familiar man in sunglasses, jeans, and a rain jacket turned toward us.

"Tucker." I touched his elbow.

Tucker patted my hand and continued texting. "Just a sec."

"Tucker, he's *here.*"

Abdallah Hussein's sunglasses hid his eyes, but I recognized the bulbous tip of his nose. He wore rubber boots that splashed the water in the square.

"Such a pleasure to meet you," said Abdallah, holding out his hand to me first. He had better manners than Luke Becker.

I took Abdallah's hand. His skin felt wet and slightly cold. He'd been waiting a while. His sunglasses slipped, and I noticed more wrinkles around his eyes and mouth up close, although he smiled nicely.

"You too," I said, giving him a once over to see if he wore the cobra fanny pack. Hard to tell under that rain jacket.

"The pleasure's all ours!" said Tucker. "Could we get you something to drink?"

Abdallah pursed his lips. "I would rather remain outside. Fewer ears."

"That's true." Tucker regarded him with respect, and we fell into step with him, with Tucker in the middle, already complimenting Abdallah's past work with museums and his research paper from four years ago.

I wore a rain jacket too, but it was semipermeable. My pants had already gotten soaked, and my hands started to sting from the rain. How long did we have to stroke this guy's ego?

Not long, as it turned out. Abdallah said, "You're too kind. I know you're wondering why Ms. Becker called me to the hospital on Wednesday."

"Absolutely," said Tucker. I nodded agreement as I blinked the rain out of my eyes.

Abdallah smiled, displaying an even set of teeth. "I am prepared to answer all your questions, as long as I'm compensated for my time, as any professional would be. We discussed a fee."

I stopped walking, even though I ended up right beside a tourist in an orange shirt taking a selfie beside a florist's display of red, white, mauve and candy floss-blue posies.

"I heard your fee," said Tucker calmly, halting beside me. "Are you able to give us some information first, as a sign of good faith?"

Abdallah stalked away from the tourist, and we followed him.

Tucker didn't even flinch as Abdallah's boots splashed water on both of us. We strode west, deeper into the square. Toward the Nile. I suspected that the rain had driven most people away, although buses continued to pull up to the station, their engines grumbling and coughing exhaust.

Abdallah turned on us. "What kind of proof do you require? I've taken the trouble to meet with you when I could have continued my research on Akhenaten."

"Very true," Tucker agreed. "We appreciate it greatly. I was curious if you're able to explain the contents of the bag, or if they're still in your possession?"

Abdallah faced us. He was a few inches taller than Tucker, which made him half a foot taller than me.

"We're students," I explained.

Abdallah's upper lip curled. "Yes, of course. Student *doctors* from *Canada.*"

I shook my head. "It doesn't mean we're rich. It means we owe people money. But we have connections, Mr. Hussein. We can help you talk to people in Canada, maybe other researchers who will appreciate your work and who might want you to help them with their exhibits, or speak on tour." Okay, I didn't know anyone like that, but Tucker might. And I could try to network with people both here and in Canada to make it so.

"That's a kind speech, but I can't eat your words. I require compensation for my time, as already discussed."

A pigeon fluttered its wings and landed on a statue in front of us, cocking its head to see if we'd feed it.

"If we do 'compensate' you, will you give us the cobra bag?" I asked him, straight out.

Abdallah sighed, pivoted toward Tucker, and held out his hand, palm up.

Tucker placed some Egyptian bills in it.

"Tucker!" I grabbed his arm, too late.

Abdallah had already palmed the bills, tallied them with a grimace, and pocketed them. "I'm sure you can do better than this, but I will offer you some information as a show of faith. Ms. Becker asked me to restore something to its rightful place."

I frowned. "That's very vague. Surely you can tell us more than that."

Abdallah scowled at me. "Your man has given me the equivalent of bus fare."

"Hey," said Tucker.

"Return bus fare," Abdallah allowed, and checked his watch. "Others have been far more generous. I should have known better than to deal with children."

"Please," said Tucker. "We're taking care of actual children. There's a little boy who's very sick in hospital. We're trying to raise money for him, so I don't have much to spare."

Abdallah raised one eyebrow, obvious even above his sunglasses. "What happened to the boy?"

I didn't want to break patient confidentiality, but this was the first question Abdallah had asked that didn't directly relate to money. "He thought he'd been bitten by a scorpion, and then he was ... "

"Suffocated. They had to dig him out of the sand," Tucker finished.

Abdallah's spine straightened. "I see. Where was the boy found?"

Tucker shook his head. "The family didn't tell me. I'm not sure. He's in hospital now, though. He survived, but he may have, ah, damaged his brain."

Abdallah checked his watch. "I have to go."

"Wait! You haven't told us about the cobra pouch." I reached for Abdallah's arm, realized I probably shouldn't touch him aside from the proffered handshake, and dropped my arms back to my sides.

"I've got it, Hope." Tucker held up another bill. A large American one.

Abdallah's nostrils flared. "'O gold! O flesh of the god!'" His hand flashed.

"Hey!" Tucker stared at his now-empty fingers. "I didn't say you could have it."

Abdallah had already pocketed the bill and turned to go. "Thank you for my fee. My children will appreciate it."

Tucker stalked alongside him, matching him stride for stride. "I could call the police. I could tell them you stole my money."

Abdallah nearly laughed. "I have your texts agreeing to the consultation fee, which exceeded your payment. If anyone should complain, it's me."

"What consultation?" I shouted, but Abdallah hailed a black car and jumped in the passenger seat. The car took off, splashing us as I took a photo of its license plate.

28

I studied the license plate photo before I showed it to Tucker. "Blurry. Did you get a better one?"

"No. Mine's even worse." Strangely, Tucker didn't sound upset as he thumbed his phone.

"Well, do you want to try and sic the police on the guy and get your U.S. dollars back, or did you really already agree to his 'fee' by text?"

"Hang on, Hope, he gave us a clue with his last line. I know it from somewhere. It's like a line from a poem. Ugh, just lost my connection."

I quickly searched the phrase and scored a direct hit, which I read aloud. "'O gold! O gold! [...] O flesh of the god! O flesh of the god! O fine gold! O fine gold!' Holy crap, that's—"

Tucker snapped his fingers. "Yes! That's what's written on the lid of Nedjemankh's tomb! I never got to see it at the Met, and they've repatriated it here."

My brain lagged a few crucial steps behind, especially this early in the morning. "Right. That's one of the artifacts you wanted to see, along with King Tut's coffins." I skimmed my screen. "Let me catch up. Nedjemankh was a senior priest at the end of the Ptolemaic Dynasty, around 100 BCE. They thought Egyptian gods were made of gold, so his two-metre wood coffin is coated in gold. His coffin was smuggled out of the country in 2011, during Arab Spring, using falsified papers."

Tucker and I exchanged a look.

"Stolen treasure," I whispered aloud. "And wait—after the IED, Muhamed translated this as 'the body of a god,' but Becker was quoting the 'flesh of the god.' Gold. 'O fine gold.' The Egyptian gods metaphorically made flesh with this gold coffin, until someone took it away."

"Not a coincidence that the Beckers came for the repatriation," said Tucker.

"You think Phillip Becker came to steal it?" I scrunched up my face. Hard to imagine an 87-year-old cat burglar and his daughter performing Mission: Impossible on a two-metre long gold coffin. Too heavy.

He half-laughed. "Seems unlikely."

"So then what?" I started pacing in the square, trying to think as my shoes stamped through the water.

What did we know for sure? Nedjemankh's coffin was stolen during a mass looting in 2011 and sold to the Met. Phillip insisted on returning to Egypt with his daughter at the same time as the coffin's repatriation. Days before the ceremony, an IED exploded near the GEM, killing him. The daughter passed on Phillip's cobra bag to Abdallah, who hinted about gold and Nedjemankh before disappearing.

Nedjemankh definitely couldn't fit in that little cobra bag. What else would?

Something so important that his daughter needed to pass it on almost upon his death bed?

Something small and crucial.

"Why did Gizelda Becker give Abdallah the cobra bag?" I asked Tucker. "He doesn't work for the GEM or the Egyptian Museum regularly. He's not a world expert. And he sure isn't trustworthy."

"It could have been Phillip Becker who trusted him," Tucker said slowly. "Phillip was the world traveller who loved Egyptian history.

Maybe Phillip even met him in 2011. Abdallah looked old enough to steal in 2011 and falsify the documents."

I nodded, thinking of the wrinkles etched in the Egyptologist's face. "That part makes sense. Phillip met Abdallah and recruited him in 2011. Phillip trusted him for years and told his daughter he was a good man. So when Phillip died on Thursday, Gizelda gave Abdallah Hussein the cobra bag. That's a big time lag, though. Abdallah left the academic track and published his last paper four years ago. So how was he making money in the meantime?"

Tucker grimaced. "Some crooked archaeologists help looters figure out what's worth selling."

"That's it!" I shook my phone. "Nedjemankh was sold in 2017. An art dealer in Paris sold it to the Met for 3.5 million euros, or 4 million dollars U.S."

"Hang on, Hope. Abdallah might have helped forge the papers in 2011, getting a small cut. I don't think he would have benefited from the big payoff."

I sighed and regarded my phone. "Yeah, if he had, he wouldn't be so desperate for a 'fee' from us 'children.'"

"Speaking of children, you think he knew anything about Hadi?"

"Hmm. Harder to tell with the sunglasses, but I got the feeling he was pimping us, not the other way around."

"Me too," said Tucker.

"I feel like ... " I hesitated. My arms itched, making me restless. "I feel like something terrible is going to happen."

Tucker paused for a minute before he answered. "Me too."

I shivered and linked my fingers with his. The rain blew into my face. I felt like I'd never get warm again.

29

My stomach dropped into my soggy running shoes when, as we waited for the bus, my phone lit up.

too late

my daddy

help

I called back right away. "Amal!"

All I got was a man speaking a string of Arabic, so I handed my phone to Tucker.

He shook his head as he listened. "This one's her dad's phone. Voice mail box is full. Try again."

I dialled again and again. No answer.

I texted Amal back before I showed Tucker our conversation.

He bent over to read the texts, so soaked that his hair stuck straight to his skull, his hair gel and hood notwithstanding. It made him look like a different person. Younger. More vulnerable. "Let me see if Rudy or someone will tell us where they transferred Hadi. We'll head down to that hospital and make sure everything's all right."

As I listened to him, my arms trembled. Even the skin felt wrong, tight and itchy, and my pants stuck to my legs in a way that made me want to rip them off in the middle of the bus station.

"I can go without you," said Tucker, reading my mind.

"I want to come," I said, rubbing my arms. "I think—I know this sounds weird, but I think the rain is bothering my skin. I have eczema, and I don't know how clean this rain is."

"Not clean," he said immediately. "The World Bank ranked Cairo as the most polluted city in the world in 2007. We'd better get you washed off."

"Isn't it bothering you?"

He shook his head. "I never get rashes. I just get shot." He glanced at me out of the corners of his eyes, grinning.

I punched his arm. "Don't joke about that! It's horrible!" Chinese people know enough not to tempt fate. Did I really have to retrain this guy?

While he pinged various people for Hadi's hospital, I headed to the bathroom to wash off.

"With bottled water," said Tucker, his eyebrows drawn together.

It seemed like a highfalutin' thing to do, but desperate times. I took a water bottle to the bus station bathroom and soaped and rinsed with tap water before rinsing with the good stuff. I offered a few Egyptian pounds to the woman who handed me paper towels while I argued with my own brain.

Amal's in trouble.

No, her dad.

Is it too late?

It's okay, we'll find Hadi, and Amal and her father are probably with him.

Don't worry.

I'm worried.

Okay, worry about this. Why did Abdallah point us toward Nedje-mankh's coffin? It's already been repatriated. An open and shut case (literally).

I don't know. What was in that cobra bag?

I don't know. Why did Gizelda Becker give it to Abdallah Hussein?

I don't know.

I dried my arms and grabbed my phone for some quick research. Looting, tomb raiding, grave robbing—whatever you want to call it— started way before Indiana Jones and Lara Croft. A papyrus from Ramses IX describes the court's punishment for thieves over 3000 years ago.

Of course governments tried to stop tomb raiding. The Geneva convention banned "illicit trade in cultural property" in 1970. In 1983, Egypt passed a law that any artifact found on their soil, obtained legally or illegally, automatically belongs to the state. In fact, Egypt lays claim to all national archaeological finds in perpetuity, unless you can supply a clear record of legal sale.

Therein lies the problem. If our suspicions were correct, all Abdullah had to do was to falsify records for Nedjemankh to get the coffin out of the country. Egyptian officials later traced its path to the United Arab Emirates, then on to Germany for restoration, before it was sold to the Met by an art dealer in Paris in July 2017.

The Parisian dealer and his husband were arrested last month. Phillip Becker and Abdallah Hussein's names never came up.

I felt the toilet attendant's eyes boring into my back, so I thanked her and stepped back into the station's hallway, where groups of people lined up for tickets, chatted with friends, and/or fiddled with their phones while they sat on their luggage.

Tucker found me first. "Hey. Rudy just sent me the hospital name. It's not that far, actually. We can be there within the hour. You think you can handle that?"

"For sure." I studied him. No rock 'n' roll sign this time. His eyes looked, well, haunted. "You okay?"

He shook his head. "I've been reading about the looting, and it's either locals who need the money—"

I nodded. I couldn't blame them.

"—or organized crime razing the sites with bulldozers, hiring archaeologists to maximize their profit, on top of what they're already making from drug smuggling and arms dealing."

I winced at the pain in his voice and touched his hand. I don't expect any better, but Tucker and Ryan still believe in human goodness.

"Bulldozers destroy everything, including the artifacts, so sometimes they use kids to reach the smallest tunnels and burial shafts."

I wrapped my arms around myself as they started to itch again. The puzzle pieces finally locked together in my brain. I wanted to scream, but somehow shoved my larynx into speech. "Maybe scorpions live down there."

He nodded.

"And definitely sand. Lots of sand that would collapse on you, especially if heavy machinery was digging out the site."

The memory of Amal's little voice rang in my ears.

My brothers can go out and work, but not me.

Hadi worked in the tunnels, either stealing artifacts for his family or for whatever crime syndicate, and now he lay close to death.

I swallowed. My throat rasped. I'd washed with my water instead of drinking it. "Okay, here's the deal. It can't get any worse. That's the good news. We've already reached the nadir of human nature. We're going to help Hadi get better. Let me call Amal again."

As we walked back to the bus stop, my phone rang and rang. I waited for the voice mail message. Instead, a little voice piped, "Dr. Sze! Oh, Dr. Sze!"

My mind spun to Dorothy calling Auntie Em in The Wizard of Oz. "What happened, Amal?"

"It's my father."

"Yes, Amal. What happened? Where are you?"

"He—he gave away his kidney."

"What?" I yelled so loudly that a group of men abruptly detoured around me, but I didn't care.

"It's too late, Dr. Sze. We owe too much money. That's what my father said. So he went to these men, these men who have always been asking him, bothering him, they know a place where you can sell your kidneys to rich people. They know the right doctors, they promised him $2000 so he could pay the hospital bill, but they dumped him in the street afterward. He's so weak. He says he has to drink, but he's—how do I say—"

In the background, I heard her father retching.

I leaned against the wall. "Oh, my God. Oh, my God."

30

"He wants to go home," whispered Amal, watching her father, now loaded into one of Cairo International Hospital's ER hallway stretchers.

"I know," I whispered back, holding her small hand, but we didn't even have his creatinine and potassium results back yet. Her dad wasn't going anywhere.

Even though her dad was sick, he wasn't sick enough to warrant the resuscitation room, or any room at all. He lay in the hallway, calling out for his son. Occasionally, he touched his left side. I'd seen the fresh, stapled incision, 15 cm long, above his anterior superior iliac spine.

At least he'd stopped vomiting, thanks in part to the bag of intravenous Ringer's lactate that Tucker and I had bought at the pharmacy en route.

"How is Hadi?" I asked Amal.

She shook her head. "They think his brain is gone."

I exhaled between my teeth. Hadi had nearly suffocated in the tunnels because his family needed money. Now his father had sold his kidney to pay Hadi's hospital bill. Yet the little boy might never recover. The whole thing made me want to cry.

Canadians donate organs. I'd heard of selling organs too, but it had seemed more like a made-up conspiracy thriller/horror movie plot than something that actually happened to living, breathing people.

The grandmother stood vigil at the dad's beside, speechless.

"Doesn't look good," Tucker whispered to me at the nursing station, after talking to the dad's doctors. "Egypt is a hub for organ trafficking. Even though it's illegal, there are plenty of scammers drugging people or coercing them into 'donating.' But if you sign all the papers, you're able to donate freely. And I think he signed everything."

I squeezed my eyes shut. "Amal said he did."

"Yemen is just about the poorest country in the world. They've got civil war. Starvation. Flooding. Half its hospitals don't work. Almost a fifth of the country has no doctor at all."

I listened in silence. I knew nothing about it. I'd even wondered if Amal had told the truth. Meanwhile, her family was literally dying of poverty.

"They come here because Egypt is one of the only countries that lets them in. Cairo is relatively affordable. You don't even need a visa if you're under 16 or over 50."

I frowned. The parents didn't look over 50, especially the mom.

"A doctor's note can get you in if you're under 50. They can write that you're coming for medical treatment. But you can't legally work here and take away jobs from Egyptians, which means you're stuck doing illegal work, harassed by authorities and getting poorer and poorer."

Scrounging for artifacts while tunnels collapse on you. Begging foreign student doctors for money.

"Selling your kidney sounds like a way out, even if it's against your beliefs. But you either get paid bupkes or you don't get paid at all. The operation might give you hepatitis. You might go into renal failure or liver failure. You can't do the physical jobs you did before because you're in chronic pain. It's a death sentence."

I recoiled, surveying Amal's father's face from 20 feet away. He'd fallen asleep during Tucker's update, too exhausted to stay awake.

"You think my father's going to die?" Amal had snuck over to listen. Her high, clear voice rang in our ears.

Tucker wrenched his head down to meet her eyes. "Oh. Amal. No, I never said that. I didn't—I mean—"

"He might die. My brother might die too. And then who will protect us? My grandmother is too old, I am too young, and my mother is pregnant."

Of course she is. I held my head as a headache drilled its way back into my temples. "Amal, we're sorry you heard that. Dr. Tucker was talking in general. We're trying to make your father as strong as possible so he can help look after you."

She stared up at me, her little chin jutting in the air. "No one is going to save us. We're going to die here, just like we would back home."

"No!" said Tucker. "I've got that fundraiser going. We'll raise more money for your dad, too. It's no trouble!"

She patted his hand. "You are a very nice man, Dr. Tucker. We thank you for everything you're doing."

Her tiny, patient resignation undid me. I cleared my throat. I refused to cry over a seven-year-old. "Amal, now that we know your brother's hospital, and your grandmother has given me permission to access your father's account here, I'll see if anyone can help pay." I'd already fired the information off to Isabelle.

Amal turned her Bambi eyes on me. "I know you're doing everything you can, Dr. Hope. We appreciate it so much. My mother wanted to tell you that."

"Where is your mother?" I looked from Amal to her father in his stretcher, her grandmother at his side. "Is she with your brother?"

Amal studied her toes and wiggled them in her sandals. "She is trying to find more money to pay for the hospitals."

"Oh, Amal. What is she doing?"

The little girl shook her head without answering.

31

MONDAY

No matter how awful we felt, we still had to work. We dragged ourselves to the Cairo International Hospital the next morning as Tucker mainlined the last of his coffee.

I stepped into the hospital lobby, but two rectangular, fluorescent white lights, mounted on stands, dazzled my retinas. What the heck?

A very polished woman in a white pantsuit stood before me and Tucker.

It wasn't Isabelle. I'd never met her in person, but I remembered Isabelle Antoun's website photo, her glasses and apple cheeks, attractive in a middle-aged, well-fed corporate way. This woman emitted hard-edged glamour, with full makeup, extensions and a blowout.

With a cameraman and professional lights already set up.

The television reporter. Karima Mansour.

Her name was emblazoned on her equipment. Even the cameraman and lighting guy had KARIMA MANSOUR lettered in white over the chests of their black T-shirts, like she was their sports team.

Or their new goddess.

I blinked at her, her cameraman and lighting guy, and then

Tucker took my arm to lead me around them. The last thing we needed from this week was a permanent record of our pain on film.

Karima sashayed to the left to block us. She applauded by clapping her left hand against her thigh before she spoke into the microphone in her right hand. "Bravo, Dr. Sze."

I hadn't spoken to her since she'd reported on the IED. Plus I hadn't done anything applause-worthy. Karima Mansour must be hallucinating. I continued to detour around her, heading for the X-ray machines.

"And Dr. John Tucker. So brave. So caring. Our audience is very impressed indeed."

Tucker touched my sleeve, silently asking me to be calm.

I took a deep breath and did a 180 to confront her, trying not to blink under the bright lights that followed me. "What are you talking about? What audience?"

"Well, you've provided quite the rollercoaster for our viewers, haven't you? You literally started off with a bomb. Then you broke our hearts with a child in peril from a possible scorpion sting. You raised our ire over the looting of national treasures. Now you've introduced us to a man willing to sacrifice his health, or even his life, for his son. What *will* you think of next?"

"No comment." With a quick step, Tucker shielded me from the camera's view and shadowed me from the light.

"But you have so many comments, Dr. Tucker. Really. You have *quite* the mouth on you." Karima Mansour batted her eyelashes, holding her microphone up to his mouth. She licked her own lips in such a sexual way, it couldn't have been clearer if she'd pretended to fellate the microphone.

Tucker bared his teeth at her.

"No," I told his back. We'd avoided major touching in public. "No one cares if we hold hands."

"You do know how to dance too," she crooned.

"Remember us waltzing in front of that cat? *One*-two-three, *one*-two-three," I whispered, but Karima Mansour's grin made my hair prickle.

What if the Egyptian Classic Continental had let Karima and her team inside our suite? They could easily drop a key card into her talons. Especially for the right price in a capitalistic society.

What if she'd spied on us from the peephole or, worse yet, from cameras planted inside our own gorgeous bedroom?

"You've made it popular again to walk like us Egyptians, don't you think?" She flexed her elbows and wrists and pointed her hands in opposite directions before she turned around to give a slight but unmistakable double-twerk under that white pantsuit.

I gasped.

Tucker gagged. I read the tension in his shoulders and the flush in the back of his neck. Meanwhile, the cameraman filmed him in technicolor, full-frontal detail.

My turn to touch Tucker's arm to calm him before I darted in front of him, screening him from view as best I could. "You're bluffing," I told Karima.

This was a conservative Muslim country. No one would spy on a couple of foreigners in the bedroom.

Well, maybe not *no one*. I could think of a perv or two.

"And if you're not bluffing, we'll sue that white pantsuit off of you," I said.

Karima Mansour unleashed her whiter-than-alabaster teeth on me. "Thank you, Dr. Sze. I'm glad you approve of my outfit. Speaking of legal cases, thank you for pointing us toward the scandal of two police officers breaking a doctor's nose. His family is so grateful."

I tried not to wince. I doubted that shy doctor relished the spotlight any more than I did. But I couldn't let her distract me. "Why did you spy on us?" I asked, straight out.

"Will you start your on-camera interview now?" She signalled her cameraman to approach. "Would you consider a little makeup? Eyebrows, mascara, eyeliner, blush, lipstick, a little evening-out of your complexion, and product in your hair. You're lucky you hardly need anything, darling."

I ignored the jab. "Darling" reminded me of Isabelle. "Why did you violate our privacy and spy on us without our permission?"

She batted her fake eyelashes at me. "I wouldn't call it spying. I'd call it fulfilling the purpose of your journey."

"*You* brought us here? Is your media outlet associated with Sarquet Industries? Or does Sarquet have a media arm?"

Karima Mansour touched her hair extensions to make sure they'd stayed in place. "Darling, please. You should see who owns Sarquet Industries."

"I looked it up. It's a privately-owned corporation."

She laughed. "And who owns the corporation?"

I glanced at Tucker, who shook his head, looking annoyed.

"It's not online," I said finally.

"Exactly. Sarquet's owner values privacy. However, I'll tell you this one for free, Dr. Sze." She beamed at her own rhyme. "Your escapades are followed all over the world. YouTube, Instagram, Facebook, Twitter, WhatsApp, Snapchat, WeChat, Weibo, and it balloons from there. One of your fans in Saudi Arabia made this trip possible."

You've got hits as far away as the Middle East, my brother Kevin had said.

All this time, I was trying to figure out Isabelle and Sarquet Industries, but someone else lay behind the curtain controlling both them and Karima Mansour. Some stalker in Saudi Arabia.

"Sarudi," I said to myself, remembering the ER chief's instant animosity. The arachnid doctor's attitude. The male doctor's contempt when I'd introduced myself to Dr. Kyrollos. The way the staff had brushed me aside during the posterior nosebleed. Even Samira's stare in the cafeteria.

Somehow, they'd known who'd sponsored my trip, or at least that he came from Saudi Arabia. To them, I wasn't a real doctor, but some rich man's toy, while they hunkered down in a war zone.

Me: I thought you wanted us to start in the emergency room right away.

Isabelle: Darling. Why would you think that?

They didn't treat Tucker with the same animosity, but I was the primary plaything. And female doctors are always first in the firing line of public opinion.

"You can tell him *this* for free." Tucker crossed his arms and angled himself in front of me, forcing Karima and the camera guy to back up.

Some guys wouldn't survive the ego death blow she'd just delivered, that they'd been flown in as a sidekick and filmed twerking in the bedroom. Not Tucker. I felt a burst of love for him as he said, "Tell him we'll sue him for more than he's worth and shred his privacy after he pulverized ours."

Karima pretended to applaud once more before she held the microphone up to his face. "Dr. Tucker, we sincerely admire your passion and value your medical expertise. Both of you have inspired our viewers to no end."

"Really?" I snapped. "Because it sounds like your buddy flew us over like a pair of stuffed animals for Show and Tell. Then he *filmed* us in our *bedroom*. How can you live with violating our fundamental human rights to make your own twisted reality TV show. We're not your zoo animals!"

My mind spun back to our first afternoon in Egypt and the IED. We'd never made it to the Giza Zoo, or Reza's grandmother, the Pyramids, or even *ta'ameya*. Just bloodshed and tears and a child suffocating in the sand.

"Dr. Sze and Dr. Tucker, please don't misunderstand me. We're eternally grateful for all that you've already accomplished. We pray for your well-being. In fact, we brought you a gift as a token of our esteem." She held out a bracelet-sized white box, tied with a glittery gold ribbon.

I refused to take it, staying behind Tucker's shoulder. "I'm sure it's illegal to spy on us. Especially in a private space, like our hotel room, or this hospital right now. Your owner might have money, but the law trumps money."

"Please. Dr. Sze. Take your gift. You've earned it." She shook the box at me.

I whirled on the cameraman and stared straight into the lens. "I don't want your 'gift.' Was *everything* a Big Brother setup? Did you— or whoever funded this—bring us to Egypt and set off an *IED?*"

"Of course not!" She blinked at me like an offended doll. "He wouldn't want to risk hurting you after all the trouble to bring you here."

"He *did* hurt me. He's not allowed to film me. He's not allowed to televise this. I never gave permission!"

"Oh, but you did." She stared down her aquiline nose at me.

"What are you talking about? I never did. Even at the hospital, when they gave me a bunch of forms about our swipe cards on the first day, I read every word."

She clicked her tongue. "It wasn't at the hospital, Dr. Sze."

"At the hotel, too."

She held out the gold-ribboned box. "Take your present."

"I don't want any presents from the stalker. What's his name?"

She stared at me. "That's not for me to say. He'll reveal his identity when he's ready to do so."

I turned back to the camera. "No problem. I'll figure out his ID when I sue him for taping me illegally."

"Tchh." When I turned back, Karima Mansour gazed down at me from her stiletto height with a pitying expression. "I doubt you have sufficient legal resources, Dr. Sze, but I'll make you a deal. You open this present, and I'll explain to you why he hasn't taped you without your consent."

"That 'present' could be another IED."

She burst into full-throated laughter and cast a sidelong view at the cameraman as he filmed every word. "First of all, I assure you that I wouldn't carry an IED with such carelessness. Secondly, I can open it for you, but we do want to capture the expression on your face."

That didn't sound promising. "Like I said, I could sue all of you."

"Dr. Sze, you have no mon-ey." She sing-songed the phrase, rhyming again. "Are you really digging yourself further into debt with a lawyer when I've promised you the answer within minutes? Your man has exquisite taste."

"Tucker does have excellent taste," I replied.

"Like Ryan Wu?"

I surged toward her before I reigned my body in.

Tucker didn't move or say a word, but his hands squeezed into fists.

Glee sparkled in her eyes as she slipped off the gold ribbon and popped open the white box's lid.

Tucker backed me away from her, protecting me with his body.

"Tucker, no!"

"You said it yourself, Hope. You don't know what's in there." He's bigger than me, and he threw out his arms when I tried to dart past him, so I peeped around his shoulder—

—and stared at a gleaming gold broach, at least an inch wide, in the shape of a fly, nested on what looked like white satin.

I hate insects. Mosquitoes dive bomb me and leave welts the size of my palm. Flies consider my food a second harvest. Ryan had cockroaches in his apartment in Ottawa when he was a poor student.

Who the fuck would want a fly as a present?

"Do you like it?" she purred.

I did my best to school my features. My Saudi stalker must have lost ten more screws if he thought this would make me like him.

"It's symbolic," she explained. "The Egyptian Pharaohs presented their best warriors with gold flies after a particularly hard-fought battle. Flies are a symbol of persistence, which is a trait he admires very much in you. Look at the detail, all rendered in 24 karat gold." Karima pointed at its outstretched wings and the individual hairs on its torso. Its spiky eyelashes reminded me of her own. "He thought you won this battle. Will you wear this for the camera?"

"No." The word jerked out of my mouth. I associated pure gold with my grandmother, who gave me a jade pendant on a 24K gold chain when I graduated from medical school.

Tucker stared at the fly, expressionless, as he probably calculated how much it was worth.

Hadi's family could use that money for their hospital debts. I could give this fly to them.

It would be so easy to reach for that box. To make myself say thank you.

Revulsion held me back, along with five words lodged in my throat.

I am not for sale.

She sighed. "Such a pity. He thought you might laugh, especially once you learned the history of it."

"He" didn't know me at all. She'd also confirmed the stalker's gender. Both things brought me tiny pieces of comfort. "You haven't answered my question about filming me illegally."

Karima Mansour laughed. "Oh, goodness. You're like an elephant. You don't forget. Yes, we have permission to film you. You gave it yourself."

"When and how?"

"At the airport. Here, I have a copy on my phone, just in case." One pink talon flicked, and she showed me a photo of a purple and white contract written in Arabic.

The contract we signed at the airport. For our cell phone SIM card. When I was jet-lagged and sprayed by toilet water and desperate to get out, I'd signed a contract I couldn't understand.

"I'm happy to send you a copy. You'll find that pages 2 and 3 are quite explicit with regard to media rights."

"Show me," said Tucker, and she pointed out the key paragraphs, switching between Arabic to English with almost palpable conde-scension.

"I'm sorry, Hope." Tucker looked pale and pinched.

"Not your fault. I'm the one who signed it." Tucker had told me it looked okay, but I should have realized his written Arabic was almost nil.

I should have asked a passer-by for help. I should have tried Google translate, even though I was conserving my phone battery to contact Sarquet Industries. I should have ...

"If it's any consolation, your platform has soared since our cover-age. Before, you were only known in Canada and a few other places. Now you're known worldwide. I have nine million followers on my Facebook page alone. You see this post?"

I closed my eyes.

Someone like Karima Mansour would never understand that I'd come to Egypt to escape from notoriety, not to add to it.

My mind flicked through my immediate priorities.

1. Get to work.

2. Make sure Tucker doesn't flip.

3. Get rid of the stalker.

I couldn't stop them from filming me, so I struck back the only way I could. "Keep the fly. Tell him I've withdrawn my permission for him to film us in public or in private. Never contact me. Don't follow me. You are dead to me." I felt a twinge at having to pay for this trip, but firmly reminded myself, *I am not for sale.*

"That goes double for me," said Tucker.

I gestured at the small, murmuring crowd that had gathered around us. Some of them captured my words on video too. "These are my witnesses, as well as you and your own cameraman. Good-bye forever."

Karima Mansour dashed after me and Tucker as we neared the X-ray machine, waving the fly box. "Dr. Sze, it's 24 karat gold!"

"I don't need any more vermin," I said. "The deal was that I'd open it, not that I'd keep it."

She fluttered her eyelashes. "He'll be so disappointed. Still, I have to thank you, Dr. Sze, for our most recent news piece."

Tucker couldn't resist. "What was that?"

"The drowning of Abdallah Hussein."

32

"*What?*" Tucker and I yelled.

Karima Mansour pouted and studied us from beneath her eyelashes. "You didn't hear? Such a tragedy. The flooding, you know."

"How do you know him? Did you verify his identity?" demanded Tucker.

Yes. I bet Egypt had more than one Abdallah Hussein. Still, I felt nauseous.

"Oh, we're aware of your connection."

They'd bugged our hotel room and bribed the staff. They'd followed us everywhere. We'd tossed them a bone by meeting at a bus station. I began scratching my arms before I could stop myself.

"Our team helped you find him, as a matter of fact. You think it was entirely the power of Twitter and your friends that uncovered his identity?" Scorn flicked up the corners of her mouth. "We broke the story and interviewed the Hussein family. He has three little children. So sad."

Tucker grasped one of my hands so tightly that I compressed my lips, but he did stop me from scratching myself as I asked, "How did a grown man drown during a flood?"

"He was electrocuted first."

I stifled a gasp. "Someone *electrocuted* him?"

She waved one stylish hand. "You must always be wary of loose electrical cables during flooding. It's not unheard-of for this to happen, although so unfortunate. Egypt really must modernize its drainage system and architecture. Then, of course, once one is electrocuted, it is so easy to drown."

Electrocuted. Drowned.

No, it wasn't a coincidence that Abdallah had been killed after he spoke to us. How did a stray electrical cable kill a healthy adult man instead of a knee-high child?

Who'd kill Abdallah Hussein?

My eye fell on the fly broach box, which Karima had passed on to the lighting director. The white box stood out against his dark skin.

I remembered the 24K gold fly's eyes. *Pestilence.*

Then I spoke to Karima Mansour, woman to woman. "I have one final story for you. This may be the most shocking one of all. But first, I need help with one very sick boy, his father, his sister, and one pregnant mother. They need medical care, education, and honest employment."

She shrugged. "Yes, I've advertised Hadi's plight in my stories. It is possible some viewers will donate to Dr. Tucker's GoFundMe, although of course we hear so many sad stories, and most Egyptians don't have spare funds. Still, we'll do our best to help you."

I leaned toward her and stared until her words died. "I will cut you out of *this* story unless you help them."

Tucker's head snapped up, and he moved to my side in silent solidarity.

She pressed her collagenized lips together. "You may have an inflated idea of a news reporter's income."

"I'm sure you could contact someone with more resources."

Her eyebrows arched. She knew I meant the stalker. "I can't make any promises on his behalf, Dr. Sze. *If* he does take on their bills as a sign of good faith, will you meet with him afterward?"

Tucker choked, but I was already shaking my head. "Never. Still, this final story could make your career. What's it going to be?"

33

WEDNESDAY

P ost-work on Wednesday, Gizelda Becker sent a car to take us to dinner. We'd offered to treat her on her last night in Cairo (hello, line of credit!), but she'd insisted on handling all the details.

Although my arms itched, I couldn't scratch them in my little black dress with a halter top, while bow-tied waiters in green vests fluttered around me and Tucker.

Fanciest restaurant of my life. Too bad I couldn't enjoy it.

A waiter pulled out my chair as I rose from our table of four to greet Gizelda Becker. I imitated Karima Mansour's confident bearing and elegant smile.

Tucker looked cool in a black shirt and black jeans, topped off with a white dinner jacket and black tie borrowed from Youssef.

"Thank you for inviting me, Dr. Sze and Dr. Tucker." Ms. Becker had braided her hair and wore some sort of flowy, eggplant-coloured boho dress.

"Thank you for coming," Tucker and I said together.

When Gizelda and I glanced at our chairs, our waiters pushed them toward the backs of our knees, ensuring that we could sit without deigning to use our hands.

Yep. Way above my student pay grade. No pressure.

A waiter topped up my water glass. Another lit the candle at the centre of an arrangement of red roses and white lilies. I thanked them, trying to look like I was accustomed to luxury instead of scrounging for egg sandwiches..

"We're so glad to see you before you fly home," Tucker said.

"My pleasure. Thank you for everything you did for my father. May I make some suggestions from the menu?"

I nodded and continued to smile as she issued instructions to the waiters, including ordering wine, something I never bother with. Hope Sze budget tip: avoid alcohol, drinks in general, appetizers, seafood, meat, and dessert if you want to eat out with minimal damage to your wallet.

Tucker chimed in with wine suggestions, and she allowed him to make the final choice.

I smiled across the table at Gizelda. "You're so generous. Maybe I should give you this to replace the one you lost." I showed Gizelda the little ankh from Noeline Momberg. "Would you like it?"

She touched her own suprasternal notch, the hollow of her neck, which lay conspicuously bare today. "Oh, you noticed my old necklace?"

"Yes, yours looked like it was made out of diamonds."

"Well. I didn't need it any more." She signalled a waiter for the red wine, sampled it, and indicated that he should pour the full glass. "Will you join me in a toast?"

Tucker amped up the charm. "Absolutely, although I thought the ankh was a symbol for everlasting life. Why wouldn't you want it any more?"

She gestured at the waiters to fill our glasses. "When you get to be my age, you realize that trinkets are meaningless."

"Yes. Life is what's important, isn't it?" I said.

"Exactly. You're young to be so wise. To life!" She lifted her glass.

I sipped and suppressed my instinct to spit it out. Too bitter for me.

Meanwhile, Tucker smiled his appreciation. "A fine vintage." He reached into the ice bucket and turned the bottle so he could read the label. "That date rings a bell. Oh, I'm sorry. Isn't 2017 the same year your mother passed away?"

She averted her head. "It is. I shouldn't have spoken so much that night. I was emotional after losing our father too."

"What happened to your mother?" he continued in a gentle voice. "Sometimes it helps to talk about it. You mentioned an autopsy."

She played with the napkin in her lap. "The report described her head injury and fractures and internal injuries. I don't understand how she went through the windshield. She always insisted on seat-belts, unlike some South Africans. She bought car seats for her grandchildren and made sure they were strapped in every time, even past the age of three."

I nodded sympathetically. I'm a seat belt devotee. If a bunch of us climb into one taxi, I'll belt two or three of us in together.

She licked her lips. Tucker and I bent forward as she dropped her voice almost to the point of inaudibility. "How could she test positive for benzodiazepines? She swore she'd never take them after one of her friends got addicted."

It is possible to trigger false positives on drug tests, but Tucker met my eyes.

"My father never got over it," she whispered. "He kept her car. Had it towed to their garage and still has it today. Refused to have it taken away. He stopped giving interviews about his mineral collection. He constantly visited our church, tithing and praying and retelling Egyptian legends. My brother said he was going mad."

Then she picked up her glass and drank. While Tucker and I murmured sympathetically, she poured herself a second and third glass of wine, topped up Tucker's glass, and ordered another bottle.

I took a deep breath. "Ms. Becker."

"Gizelda."

"Gizelda, I know this is a difficult time, but did you hear what happened to Abdallah Hussein?"

She sloshed her wine onto the table, staining the white tablecloth. A waiter instantly dropped a white napkin over the splotch before retreating.

"He was electrocuted first," I said. "Then he drowned in the flood-waters around his home. His wife and three little children are staying with relatives for now. They say it could have been a stray electrical cable, but I find it strange that no other family members or neighbors were electrocuted or drowned. Only Abdallah."

"Oh no." She held her head. "Oh, God. Jesus, help me. No, no, no, no, no."

O gold! O gold! O flesh of the god!

Tucker said, in a gentler voice, "You gave him your father's cobra bag. Could you please confirm its contents?"

She wouldn't look up.

"Maybe this would help?" I held up a screenshot on my phone, a photo of the mummified hand gifted from Harold Carter to Sir Bruce Ingram.

She covered her face, but Tucker intoned, "'Cursed be he who moves my body. To him shall come fire, water, and pestilence.'"

"Pestilence? What on earth are you talking about?" demanded a man striding across the room.

34

W e all stared up at the oversized man who loomed over us. His shadow blocked Tucker's face, but as I gazed up at him, I noticed a red spot on his left jaw, near the temporomandibular joint.

"Hello, Mr. Becker," said Tucker evenly. "So glad you could make it. Yes, we were talking about pestilence." Tucker reached into the breast pocket of his borrowed suit jacket and opened up a small white box, revealing the 24-carat gold fly.

"Luke," the man said gruffly, dropping into the last seat of the table, between Tucker and Gizelda and across from me. Luke, too, wore a suit jacket, although his was soft grey wool and looked tailored to minimize his bulk. He poured himself a glass of wine from the new bottle, tasted it, and gritted his teeth. "What is this shit? Bring me your beer."

"Right away, sir," said the closest waiter.

I cradled the fly broach in my left hand like I'd never seen it before. "That's wild."

"Can I see that?" Luke reached for the fly broach, but I cupped it in my left hand, swinging it toward Gizelda, who leaned away from it.

"Where did you get that?" Luke beckoned me with his hand as he followed the broach with his eyes. That gave me a better look at the red spot on his cheek. It was more like a swelling. A dental abscess.

I raised my eyebrows at Tucker and slid the fly to the right, to my guy, who tucked it back into his jacket pocket with practiced ease. "Hang on. Did I ever tell you that I do magic tricks?"

Luke harrumphed and tossed back some of the Sakara Gold beer newly placed in front of him. "No."

"Yeah. I used to perform at schools and restaurants. The kids would clap their hands and tell me how awesome I was. I never made four million dollars, though."

Luke swivelled his bulk to face Tucker. "What are you saying?"

"The Paris art dealer sold the coffin of Nedjemankh to the Met in July 2017 for 3.5 million euros, or very close to four million U.S. dollars," I told him. "Now, we realize that you and your father wouldn't have made four million. You'd have to pay off the looters and the guards and Abdallah Hussein, or whoever else falsified the documents, plus the art dealer. Still. Four million U.S."

"You're insane." Luke stood, his massive knees knocking the table and rattling the wine glasses. "Let's go, Gizelda."

She stared up at him before she waved an index finger at the wine bottle label. "Luke, look. This wine is from 2017."

He sighed and reached for her elbow to help her up. "What of it?"

She evaded his grasp. "That's the year our family suddenly came into more money."

He shrugged. "Lots of things happened in 2017. Let's go."

She tucked her elbows against her chest. "You and Father flew to Paris at the end of June and stayed through to July. I remember that. Quite soon after, Father started building the home museum for his mineral collection."

Luke snorted. "He loved those rocks."

"He loved history. He loved art. And most of all, he loved our mother. Mother was our company accountant until July 2017, when you said we should hire an outside firm. As soon as she died, you hired the books out to Krygers."

"Yes, yes, water under the bridge. Let's go, or I'll leave without you."

The waiter reappeared with another beer on a white-napkined tray.

Luke towered over him. "Get out of my way!"

I stood up, too, drawing his eye. "Yes, so sad that your accountant mother died after coming to your house. Did you sabotage her car? Or drug her so much that she couldn't remember how to put on her seatbelt? Or both?"

"Hope!" Tucker bounded to his feet.

Luke shoved his red face in mine, across the table. "You're lucky you're a woman in a public place."

I stared right back into his crazy eyes. "Why, are you going to kill me like you killed your mother and Abdallah Hussein when they asked you too many questions about your artifacts? Plus the kids dying to dig them up? You can just say yes. The real question is how you engineered the IED that killed your father. So interesting that the last bomb that killed tourists in Egypt took place in 2017. The year of your giant payout."

Luke reached under his suit jacket and seized a gun from his shoulder holster.

I hit the ground, bashing both knees before I landed on my stomach, hollering, "Tucker!"

He landed a split second after me, as police officers stampeded the room and Karima Mansour's majestic voice cut through the air.

"Luke Becker, a murderer unmasked! Broadcasting live from the Egyptian Classic Continental!"

35

"That story may break the Internet," said Karima Mansour, after the police had tackled Luke Becker and led him away before he fired a single shot.

"With any luck," said Tucker, holding up his glass for Gizelda. She filled it, her hands only trembling a little.

Karima dropped into Luke Becker's seat and shook out her hair extensions. "I spoke to the police. They interviewed the widow of Abdallah Hussein, who positively identified Luke, or Luca, Becker as the man who came to their house and argued with her husband before leading him outside and—" She gestured with her free hand.

Somehow electrocuting and drowning him. I closed my eyes. Abdallah Hussein had figured out Hadi's fate and tried to blackmail Luke Becker over it, only to end up a victim himself.

"Hadi's family isn't willing to speak on camera yet, but I think they will, with a little incentive." Karima smiled and sipped the last of our wine.

Tucker cleared his throat, glancing at Gizelda Becker.

Gizelda's eyes shone with unshed tears, but she shook her head at Tucker. "Don't worry about me. I want justice served. If my brother killed Abdallah Hussein, and if he's responsible for a child nearly suffocating, I want to know about it."

"All of you will need to join us at the station to make a statement," said an older police officer.

"Please, I need to recover for a minute," said Gizelda, clinging to her wine glass.

Karima Mansour switched to Arabic to charm the officer into agreeing to a short reprieve. Then she ordered more wine.

I glanced down at my empty plate. I would have loved to get in a few bites before my police statement.

"Your appetizer is coming, madam. We'll pack up the rest for you to take with you," said a waiter.

Truly the best service of my life. I grinned at him as I unhooked the microphone from my collar and placed it on the table for Karima Mansour. "Thanks so much to you and your team. Gizelda, you were so brave."

Gizelda shook her head. "You've answered a lot of questions for me already. This is my treat. I gave the staff my credit card information."

"Oh, Gizelda ... "

"It's the least I can do. It won't bring back our mother, of course." Her voice shook. "I always wondered what had happened, and why my father changed so much even before her death. I'll hire a fleet of forensic accountants to comb through our company books. I'll look through our father's papers as well. Now that I realize that a cat with an ♀ is his symbol for Nedjemankh, I can decipher his records."

I'd wondered about that. I couldn't remember the name Nedjemankh myself, until I parsed it into Nedjem—sweetness, like the cats who'd repeatedly visited me—and ankh, which meant life. Once I started looking for the ankh, I saw it everywhere, including in King Tut-ankh-amun.

"Good idea," said Tucker. "I bet that's why your father kept her car. He wondered if there might have been foul play, but couldn't bring himself to confront your brother. You can have the car checked if you feel up to it."

Gizelda touched her temples. "I know my father wasn't a saint. He must have been the instigator, or at least involved, with the looting in 2011 and the coffin sale in 2017. But he did try to give back that hand in the cobra pouch. He was going to present it to the Grand Egyptian Museum. He was meeting with staff and trying to figure out the best way to return it, but that IED killed him first." She took a deep breath. "I entrusted the hand to Abdallah. He promised he'd take care of it for me in exchange for my necklace and some money to bribe officials."

I exhaled. It was possible that Abdallah had returned the hand. It was also possible that he'd pocketed her cash and diamond ankh and hung onto the hand to resell it before dying of fire (electrocution) and floods (drowning).

"And pestilence," I said aloud, remembering Luke's dental abscess. At least one source had described the infected spot sitting on Lord Carnarvon's left cheek.

I'm a doctor. I believe in science. However, for the first time, legends and history had led me to solving this crooked case. I wouldn't cry if that dental abscess expanded, disseminated, and killed Luke Becker in jail.

"How did you figure out my brother's role?" asked Gizelda.

"Your father was giving you clues," I said. "The story about the mongoose and the cobra—when he smuggled antiquities, your father probably imagined himself as the mongoose fighting with the cobra, the symbol of the pharaohs."

"And his nickname was Meerkat, which is a type of mongoose in South Africa," Tucker said. "Meerkats are excellent diggers, building tunnels underground. Pretty symbolic for someone digging treasure out of tombs."

Treasure. I touched his hand. Tucker had figured that out by himself, since I hadn't bothered to look up meerkats. Then I turned to Gizelda. "Meerkat was his nickname as a student athlete. Do you think he started stealing artifacts back then?"

Gizelda lowered her head. "I'm afraid I don't know. My mother kept the books at home and at work, not me. Father always did love Egyptian heritage. In those days, they didn't have the same kind of rules."

They'd had rules since at least 1970. And Phillip Becker had "loved" Egyptian heritage so much that he'd ripped it out of the earth, away from its people, and sold it for a multimillion dollar profit.

I didn't buy the "back in the day" argument. Even if kids like Hadi hadn't died at his feet, Phillip Becker must've known of the blood shed for his precious "treasures."

A few months ago, I would have told her so. Tonight, I surveyed Gizelda Becker's lined, weary face and realized that she was now an orphan with a killer brother. Whatever her father had done, he'd died for it. We'd never know the whole truth. And we had to keep her on our side to prosecute her brother.

Sometimes a scorpion must sting in order to eat or to defend herself. And sometimes a goddess wields her scorpion power in order to heal and to help a person breathe.

So I asked a different question. "You remember that after the IED, you said Phillip was all mixed up, praying and calling for Luke and asking the time? One of our friends suggested that your father might have been citing something like Luke 13:5."

Tucker bowed his head. "'I tell you, no! But unless you repent, you too will all perish.'" In addition to feeding us shawarma, Maryam had solved *L 12:15,* that tiny clue in the red book, the first minute we met.

Gizelda's jaw dropped open. It took her a few seconds to speak. "I thought he was praying."

Either that, or Mr. Becker had been naming his own son, Luke, as the instigator of the bombing and/or the inheritor of his tomb raiding empire. That, too, I'd leave to the police. I only had one more question. "Did I hear you say Krygers to your brother?"

Gizelda hesitated before she nodded. "Yes, it's the expensive accounting firm my brother hired to take over the books after our mother died."

"That's the word your father was saying. I thought it was Kruger, like Kruger National Park." Like the Kruger Millions. Instead, Mr. Becker had named the last of his enemies before he died.

Gizelda bit her lip and lowered her head. "My father told me everything, and I didn't understand. I was holding his head, I was trying to stop the bleeding, but I didn't *listen.*"

"Don't blame yourself. We didn't understand it either," said Tucker. He held up his phone. "It's interesting, though. Looks like *krygers* is Afrikaans for 'warrior.' That could be another interpretation of your father's words."

Gizelda placed a hand on her chest. For one terrible second, I thought she'd throw up, but the moment passed, and she said, "It makes no sense. My father wasted so much time on this trip telling me about Egyptian gods and goddesses. Osiris, Isis, Anubis, Bata ... "

I nodded and said, as gently as possible, "The legends of Osiris, Isis, Set, Nephthys, and Horus, as well as Anubis and Bata, are really stories about usurping power from the rightful king."

"With a war between the siblings before good finally triumphs," Tucker said. "Your father fed you clues, using allegories to show how your brother fought him for control the company and the Becker fortune."

Gizelda's eyes filled with tears. "Stubborn old man. Why couldn't he tell me directly?"

I touched her weathered hand. "Sometimes it's easier to speak indirectly. I think the smuggling would be really hard to confess after what, 70 years?"

"Especially if your dad drafted your brother into the business and might have gotten your mother killed," said Tucker.

Gizelda's shoulders stiffened. She grabbed a napkin to cover her sobs.

I tried to soften the blow. "Your dad knew he might lose you too. You were the only loyal family he had left. So he planned this trip with you, trying to stay safe by keeping with the group." I hesitated. "I wonder if he was even behind Nedjemankh's repatriation, letting the Egyptian authorities know that the documents were forged. So that the coffin of Nedjemankh would make it safely home before he returned the hand and made a clean breast of things."

Gizelda shook her head. "He would *never* be clean." She turned to Karima Mansour. "I saw your report about the poor little boy and the other children who were injured or killed digging for 'treasures.'" Her mouth twisted. "I'll take Luca to court for damages, and I'll see what I can do for the children."

"Thank you," said Karima, raising her glass of wine in appreciation.

I squirmed in my chair. Not to make this a total downer, but I couldn't leave it like that. "The whole family's in trouble. Hadi's father donated his kidney to try and raise money. Hadi's pregnant mother was beaten last night."

"Oh, goodness. Is that another story?" Karima's eyes gleamed, reflecting the candlelight.

Tucker shook his head. "The mom won't talk about it. She won't even go to the hospital."

The mother wouldn't risk another hospital bill. She'd returned to Hadi's side, limping and refusing to speak.

Gizelda's forehead wrinkled as she repeated, "I'll do what I can."

"They're both doing better today, *In'sha'Allah*," said Tucker, and we all relaxed.

"*In'sha'Allah*," I repeated. I hoped Hadi and his family could relax and heal. I hoped that my stalker, Gizelda Becker, generous Canadians and Egyptians, or some magic combination of all of the above, would join forces to help at least this one family.

Tucker slid the fly box toward Karima, who palmed it. Maybe the 24K gold fly would make its way back to the stalker. Or maybe Karima and her cameraman would put it to good use. Either way, I wanted no part of that pestilence.

"Let me know if we can help," I told Gizelda. Historically, Set had battled Osiris and Horus with Isis in the wings.

In the 21st century, we'd pit Isis directly against Set. Maybe I could play Serket and help Isis breathe while she prepared for war.

"You've already helped so much, darling," Gizelda said.

Tucker called me a scorpion goddess. Every woman in Egypt called me darling. So what was I? The lady or the tiger? The scorpion or the darling? The sister or the wife?

Was it possible to say "all of the above"? I threw my head back and laughed, feeling the soft napkin in my lap and Tucker's eyes on mine.

Tucker smiled and squeezed my hand before he leaned toward Gizelda. "Your father was treated at KMT Hospital. That's the ancient name for Egypt, which was drawn like this." Tucker pulled out Gizelda's red notebook and laid a piece of paper on top. Then he drew some shapes that looked vaguely familiar, including a bird, on the paper. "KMT also means 'shield' or 'conclusion.' Although I know this is a difficult time for you, I can't help thinking it's symbolic that your father did try to make amends at the end, at his conclusion. That should be good for his *Ma'at,* right? *Ma'at* means balance and order and putting things to rights."

Gizelda downed some more wine. "Father did talk about *Ma'at.* He said that in the afterlife, she's the goddess who weighs your heart against a feather on the scales of justice."

"We'll all pray for him," Karima assured her. "Don't worry."

If an afterlife existed, would Phillip Becker's 11th hour turnaround be enough? Suddenly, I remembered him saying, *My heart is heavy. It weighs too much.*

I'd assumed he had chest pain from the trauma and/or ischemia. But what if, at the end of your life, a goddess really did greet you in Osiris's Hall of Truth to weigh your heart on a golden scale against *Ma'at's* white ostrich feather?

If that organ weighed more than the feather, as Amal had pointed out, your heart was tossed on the ground and devoured by Ammut, the monster. And then you would cease to exist.

What if I'd witnessed that moment of weighing before Mr. Becker lost consciousness?

Boy. I'd better start living righteously from this second forward.

On the other hand, one other quote rang in my mind, the second quote Tori had written on a card for us: "Fear does not prevent death, it prevents life."

I exhaled and met Tucker's eyes across the white tablecloth. Death surrounded us.

And yet I rejected fear.

I chose to live.
I chose to love.
I chose, as Elizabeth Barrett Browning wrote,
A place to stand and love in for a day,
With darkness and the death-hour rounding it.

AFTERWORD

On May 19th, 2019, my tour group posed near the Giza Pyramids when they heard an explosion.

"What was that?" One of them jumped. She could feel the earth tremble.

"Oh, nothing," said the tour guide, hurrying them along.

The IED, planted in a car near the Grand Egyptian Museum, hit a bus carrying 28 people, 25 of whom were tourists from South Africa (https://www.bbc.com/news/world-middle-east-48328793).

Fortunately, no one died, although 17 were injured, including two who suffered eye trauma.

This is the inciting incident for *Scorpion Scheme.*

Most other details are true, too, if rearranged: the retaliation against Hasm; the bomb that killed three Vietnamese tourists and an Egyptian tour guide; the repatriation; the children dying underground; the organ trade; the political unrest; even the sneaky toilet and fake palm trees.

Yet I felt safe during my trip. I walked in the Valley of Kings and Queens. I cruised down the Nile. I swam in the Red Sea.

My friends thanked me for my positive portrayal of the Middle East on social media, because Western media emphasizes the danger.

So I want to stress that, in 2019, the vast majority of tourists had absolutely no trouble visiting Egypt. And I, for one, relished discovering an entire civilization with thousands of years of history.

However, on my outbound flight from Vienna to Cairo, I chatted with a seat mate who informed me of the bombing we'd missed. I assumed he was joking.

"No. It was a bomb. You can read about it yourself when we land."

"Really?" I'd joined the tour late so I could celebrate my son's birthday with him, which meant I was a continent away when the IED went off. I thought, *Wow. My son protected me.*

What a fluke. Is this what happens? Random things tilt us on the knife edge between an indulgent vacation and losing our eyesight?

Yes. That's become even more clear in 2020. In case you're reading *Scorpion Scheme* in the future, this is the hardest year our planet has collectively faced in my lifetime. We've recorded 36,778,228 cases of COVID-19, with 1,066,391 deaths as of October 9th.

I'm still practicing as an emergency physician and a hospitalist looking after admitted patients. We brace for the next wave as I write.

Which reshaped *Scorpion Scheme* in real time. I'm not writing about the pandemic because it's not entertaining to me. Literally, doctors, nurses, war veterans, children, cancer patients, writers, artists, musicians, scientists, parents, grandparents, athletes, and more have been killed by SARS-CoV-2, taking a disproportionate toll on the poor and people of colour.

I want to escape that right now. So *Scorpion Scheme* contains very little on-page violence and more food, myths, dancing, and getting busy.

Why?

'Cause Hope needs it.

Because I need it.

I have only two small inklings of what will happen next to Hope, Tucker, and Ryan. I only know that they'll keep on living, loving, fighting crime, and fighting each other.

Keep reading. Keep fighting. Keep dreaming. We need you.

ACKNOWLEDGMENTS

Enormous gratitude to everyone who helped shape *Scorpion Scheme,* my first pandemic book.

Dr. Kyrollos explained a lot of crucial details about Egypt, including the lack of scorpions in Cairo (oops);

Dr. Monica Hanna, a real Egyptian archaeologist, answered a question that changed a crucial scene;

RN Margaret MacDonald managed to edit even though she came out of retirement to juggle telehealth and to assist with three grandchildren, including two new grandbabies;

Dr. M zeroed in on my Arabic and food misdirections, with help from Yusra Jomha;

Drs. Najat Al-Refaie Sasani, K, H, Y, W, and Y kindly offered to help;

I received some Arabic guidance from pharmacist George Nagy and several kind people in Discord's Arabic Learning Centre: رَشِيـدُ بْنُ دِرْهَـم, Arabic Tesla, coldasice, and Agent P;

Many books and podcasts proved invaluable, including the Egypt Travel Podcast and Dominic Perry's The History of Egypt podcast;

My wonderful beta readers continued wonderful-ling;

My sharp-eyed, quick-witted readers voted on titles and potential cover photos; and

Chris McIntosh created the final title.

All faults are my own.

Considering COVID-19, this is a group win for 2020.

ABOUT THE AUTHOR

Melissa Yi is an emergency doctor with an award-winning writing career.

She believes in health, humour, hard work, and hoorays.

Win a free Hope novella by joining the KamikaSze newsletter on Melissa's website, www.myi.ninja

Earn literary karma by leaving a positive review at your favourite retailer.

And rock on.

amazon.com/author/myi

facebook.com/MelissaYiYuanInnes

twitter.com/dr_sassy

bookbub.com/authors/melissa-yi

instagram.com/melissa.yuaninnes

pinterest.com/melissayi_

ALSO BY MELISSA YI

Code Blues (Hope Sze 1)

Notorious D.O.C. (Hope Sze 2)

Family Medicine (essay & Hope Sze novella combining the short stories *Cain and Abel, Trouble and Strife, and Butcher's Hook*, which are also available separately)

Terminally Ill (Hope Sze 3)

Student Body (Hope Sze novella post-Terminally Ill; includes radio drama *No Air*)

Blood Diamonds (Hope Sze short story)

The Sin Eaters (Hope Sze short story)

Stockholm Syndrome (Hope Sze 4)

Human Remains (Hope Sze 5)

Blue Christmas (Hope Sze short story)

Death Flight (Hope Sze 6)

Graveyard Shift (Hope Sze 7)

Scorpion Scheme (Hope Sze 8)

More mystery & romance novels by Melissa Yi

The Italian School for Assassins *(Octavia & Dario Killer School Mystery 1)*

The Goa Yoga School of Slayers *(Octavia & Dario Killer School Mystery 2)*

Wolf Ice

High School Hit List

The List

Dancing Through the Chaos

Unfeeling Doctor Series (Melissa Yuan-Innes)

The Most Unfeeling Doctor in the World and Other True Tales From the Emergency Room (Unfeeling Doctor #1)

The Unfeeling Doctor, Unplugged: More True Tales From Med School and Beyond (Unfeeling Doctor #2)

The Unfeeling Wannabe Surgeon: A Doctor's Medical School Memoir (Unfeeling Doctor #3)

The Unfeeling Thousandaire: How I Made $10,000 Indie Publishing and You Can, Too! (Unfeeling Doctor #4)

Buddhish: Exploring Buddhism in a Time of Grief: One Doctor's Story (Unfeeling Doctor #5)

The Unfeeling Doctor Betwixt Birthing Babies: Poems About Love, Loss, and More Love (Unfeeling Doctor #6)

The Knowledgeable Lion: Poems and Prose by the Unfeeling Doctor in Africa (Unfeeling Doctor #7)

Fifty Shades of Grey's Anatomy: The Unfeeling Doctor's Fresh Confessions from the Emergency Room (Unfeeling Doctor #8)

Broken Bones: New True Noir Essays From the Emergency Room by the Most Unfeeling Doctor in the World (Unfeeling Doctor #9)

The Emergency Doctor's Guide Series (Melissa Yuan-Innes)

The Emergency Doctor's Guide to a Pain-Free Back: Fast Tips and Exercises for Healing and Relief

The Emergency Doctor's Guide to Healing Dry Eyes